The Home Front

July - August 1941

A Misfit Squadron Book

Simon Brading

First published 2024

ISBN: 978-1-917470-08-7

THE
LONG WAY HOME

JULY – AUGUST 1941

THE LONG WAY HOME

The following is an excerpt from the personal diary of Chastity Arrowsmith and gives an account of the retreat from Alexandria.

Written as it is by someone who took part in the retreat, but who was not a part of the land journey itself, having spent the entire time in the air, it provides a unique perspective, being less dry and logistical than some accounts and dealing less with heat and exhaustion than others. Her prose is also rather better than that of most first-hand witnesses, being heavily influenced by her reading material at the time - the works of a close personal friend of hers: George Orwell.

The role of Acting Aviator Lieutenant Arrowsmith and the official and unofficial members of 112 Squadron, based in Alexandria, is largely played down in the accounts written by those on the ground. Indeed, she herself greatly understates her and her fellow pilots' heroism. However, later analysis suggests that their contribution was vital and perhaps the deciding factor in the success or failure of the retreat.

F. Featherstonehaugh - Misfit Squadron during The Hiatus. 1941.

DAY 1

RAC Aboukir. Alexandria.
First light. 29th July 1941.
Clear skies. 23°. Wind NW 10 knots.

The evacuation of Alexandria and its surrounds is almost complete. Every single military facility, every camp, base, dock, warehouse, factory, gun emplacement, pillbox, everything where a British or allied soldier, sailor or airman was stationed was abandoned at midnight last night. Nothing has been left behind to aid the enemy and, in almost all cases, the facilities themselves have been mined and will be blown apart as or before they arrive. The only remaining British forces are at RAC Aboukir and they consist solely of the surviving aircraft and pilots of 112 Squadron (all 7 of us) and a single lorry, which will carry the 7 fitters who have remained behind to help with the aircraft, as well as the sapper officer who will arm the charges set on the airfield as they leave.

So, after weeks of intercepting Coalition bombers on a regular as clockwork twice-daily basis, this morning we have something different to do. Our orders are twofold: firstly, to act as if we are still based at Aboukir and all is as it should be, and, secondly, to distract the Prussian and Italian aircraft however we can and hopefully prevent them from spotting the retreat (although there isn't much hope of that, as a convoy the size of ours will undoubtedly throw up a cloud of dust that could probably be spotted from their bases in Cyprus). Once we have done what we can we are to race to rendezvous with the convoy at the staging point. There we will rearm and rewind and be ready to engage with any enemy aircraft that comes looking for us.

Egypt, a friend of Britain since the days of the empire, is to be left to the tender mercies of the Prussians. The locals understand the necessity, but are apprehensive, to say the least - they have seen how the Italians, in particular, treat countries that they conquer. I have to believe that the situation will only be temporary, but, as things are going in this war, that might be a vain hope.

Giza, nr. Cairo.
10 a.m.
Clear skies. 33°. Wind NW 5 knots.

Despite the fact that we'd been keeping a close eye on the build-up of ships and materiel in Cyprus in preparation for the invasion of Egypt, it was definitely a shock seeing all those vessels steaming at full pelt towards Alexandria. We didn't have much time to contemplate the awe and majesty of the Coalition fleet, though, being rather more preoccupied by the swarm of fighters escorting them.

Our attempts to draw them off failed and so Squadron Leader Pendergast decided that a swift attack and then a judicious retreat would be the best course of action. We climbed, causing the enemy to split in two - one half mirroring us, while the rest stayed to cover the ships - then, when the time was right, we feigned an attack on the top group. At the last second, though, we dived under them and onto the lower group. We passed through, causing chaos and damaging several - I believe I made two kills, but was unable to confirm them - but did not stay to dogfight, instead using our speed to disengage and race for Aboukir.

A few of the enemy fighters from the top group gave chase, but gave up very quickly, most likely not wanting to run the gauntlet of the anti-aircraft guns surrounding the airfield, having no way to know that those guns were even now bouncing across the desert many miles away.

We weren't returning to the airfield, of course, but flew straight past at full unwind, heading south-west. Only when we'd gone a further fifty miles and were sure that there was no pursuit and that nobody could see us did we turn east and make for the staging point.

That far from Alexandria the countryside is featureless and has no landmarks, but there was no need for any fancy feats of navigation; we could see our rendezvous point from more than a dozen miles away and, in just over half an hour since we'd engaged the fighters escorting the invasion fleet, we landed on a hastily-cleared patch of land, in the shadow cast by the largest of the pyramids at Giza.

Now, a couple of hours later, the evacuation has been completed, the last of the lorries having arrived at the staging point here beneath the pyramids at shortly after ten, having been delayed for an hour by a puncture, of all things. There is no time to rest, though, as the Prussians will be aware by now that we are no longer there, so the convoy has already moved out again. Pursuit should take some time to organise, though, especially as the port and airfield were both destroyed as we left. As for the squadron - we will be on overwatch, so to speak, flying high above the pyramids and keeping an eye out for any attempt to catch the convoy.

Nr. Ras Shukeir, Gulf of Suez.
8 p.m. Wind SE 8 knots.

It has been a long day for everyone, but all the hard work and subterfuge have paid off. The entirety of the British forces stationed in Egypt (all that are left in Africa, in fact, at least as far as we know), with all the men and women that have been taken in after the defeats of Cyprus and Greece, have arrived safely at the embarkation point on the shore of the Gulf of Suez.

A signal was received an hour or so ago from the evacuation fleet, that they were staged in the Red Sea out of sight of shore and were ready to enter the mouth of the gulf as soon as it was dark. It is just over sixty miles from there to the bay just north of the town of Ras Shukeir and, if all goes well, they should be with us by two in the morning.

Equipment is replaceable, men and women are not, so all the vehicles and what little remains of the stores will be destroyed so that the boarding can be carried out as quickly as possible. I will be sorry to consign my battered and broken, but still willing, Harridan to the flames; she has carried me through many a hard battle and gotten me out of quite a few tight scrapes, but there is no other choice. I will take a little something as a souvenir - perhaps the artificial horizon instrument, which hasn't worked for the last three weeks.

I have no idea when I will be able to get back to England and the Misfits. With the Prussian undersea boats such a menace, there aren't many convoys from India to Britain, if indeed we are taken there and not to either South Africa or even Australia. I am hopeful that there will be a berth available on another undersea boat heading to England at some time, though. It's not that I haven't been able to accomplish anything in a regular RAC squadron and wouldn't be useful wherever I were to be sent, but I know I would be able to accomplish more with the Misfits.

DAY 2

Nr. Ras Shukeir, Gulf of Suez.
5 a.m. 30th July 1941.
Clear skies. 24°. Wind SE 10 knots.
What is it they say about the best laid plans?

The evacuation fleet was waylaid as it sailed up the Red Sea. Whether the Prussians were lying in wait, had intercepted their signals and rushed to cut them off, or had simply happened on them by chance we will probably never know, but it is immaterial now; the fact is that those ships that weren't sunk were forced away and will not be coming back.

With escape via the Red Sea to the east now unavailable, Italians occupying Abyssinia to the south and Coalition forces occupying Alexandria to the north and most likely already moving towards us, the only option left, beyond the unthinkable, is west.

With Egypt friendly, food and water, at least, are replenishable resources, but other supplies are sparse. The desert is a harsh taskmaster and, while the people should cope well enough, it will be hard on our machinery. Hopefully, though, the Prussians will not spot us slinking away and the desert will be all that we have to contend with - we have more than 2500 miles to travel before we get to the Atlantic and that is going to be hard enough, without having to fight a rearguard action the whole way.

The convoy was hastily reassembled as soon as the news came in at 3 in the morning and moved out as soon as it could, initially much less organised than it had been yesterday. The squadron remained behind, though, and will fly cover during the day - we cannot safely takeoff and land in the dark and we are not much use if we can't see anything.

Kharga Oasis.
7 p.m.
Clear skies. 35°. Wind SW 5 knots.
The convoy made good time today, first heading south in order to cross the Nile near Qena before striking out due west for Kharga Oasis, where we have stopped for a few hours rest.

Scouts were sent into Qena as we passed, in order to secure whatever supplies they could from local tradesmen. They managed to obtain food, drink and a small stock of assorted tires, which will be invaluable as the miles pass, but there was little to be had in the way of machine oil, unfortunately.

The squadron flew several sorties during the day, shadowing fifty or so miles behind the convoy and flying as high as visibility would permit in order to scour the sands for any signs of an organised pursuit, but we saw none.

Conditions in the vehicles must be hellish, with temperatures reaching 40° or more, but there are no complaints to be heard and morale is high. There seems to be almost a holiday camp atmosphere, in fact, with songs and improvised entertainments, as well as quite a few bottles being passed around. This is most likely due to the rather widespread belief that we have made a clean getaway, reinforced by the fact that the squadron spotted nobody today. It is, of course, far too early to tell for sure whether this is true or not, but that hasn't stopped the celebrations.

DAY 3

Kharga Oasis.
8 a.m. 31st July 1941.
Clear skies. 30°. Wind SW 3 knots.

Once again the squadron has been abandoned at the camp site by the convoy, which moved on in the early hours of the morning while it was still dark.

Now that we are heading out into the desert, things become a bit more complicated. While it is easy enough for us to follow the convoy - the tracks they make are obvious enough without taking into consideration the large cloud of dust - finding somewhere for us to land and rewind is not such a simple prospect. The scouts have to find a suitably large space without too much in the way of obstructions and then our ground crews have to clear it and use the steamroller to compact and flatten it. It is backbreaking work and, understandably, they want to do it as few times as possible, so the plan is for somewhere suitable to be found approximately half-way between where the convoy started and where it will stop for the night. The scouts and ground crew will be forging into unknown territory, so they will take with them some of the fighting force - fully a quarter of the tanks and armoured autocars - as protection, leaving the slower moving vehicles - the more heavily laden lorries, the artillery pieces and the various utility vehicles - slightly more exposed as a result.

Whatever the risks and hardships for the advance party, they are worth it; the warning the squadron will give in the event that the

Prussians do catch up, will allow the forces to recombine and a defensible position to be found.

Approx. 250 miles west of Kharga Oasis
10 p.m.
Clear skies. 15°. Wind SW 10 knots.
Spirits are still buoyed by the fact that there is still no sign of the enemy, but we are now more than two hundred and fifty miles from the oasis, deep into the desert and it is hot and dry and perfectly inhospitable and the mood has turned a bit more sober. There are still those who are laughing and joking, but as the moisture burns out of their mouths they fall increasingly silent and sleep is now treasured more highly than camaraderie or drink.

DAY 5

Harat Zuwayyah Oasis, Libya.
7 a.m. 2nd August 1941.
Clear skies. 30°. Wind SE 8 knots.

I left my diary in my kitbag by mistake yesterday, but there was nothing much to report anyway. As the convoy crossed a line on a map and entered Libya, the squadron flew three sorties and saw nothing except a possible sand storm far to the south and maybe a camel train in the distance to the north-west. There was nothing to relieve the monotony, in fact, not a bird, nor a cloud, and I have given up hope of seeing any interesting mirages, like there are in adventure stories.

Boredom means safety, though, and I would much rather be bored than lose lives.

What we are losing, however, is vehicles. Alexandria had been cut off from supplies for months, which means that the vehicles have had to do without replacement parts far longer than they should have. Every day several are abandoned in the path of the retreat, guiding us back to the convoy like breadcrumbs. At the moment, the situation is not critical. There are enough lorries to carry our dwindling stock of supplies and the tanks and armoured cars can provide secure, if uncomfortable, perches for the men and women left without dedicated transport. However, we are only at the beginning of our exodus and there are many more miles to go.

Waw an Namus, Libya.

9 p.m.
Clear skies. 32°. Wind NE 10 knots.

We suffered our first casualty today: our commanding officer, Squadron Leader Pendergast. He seemed to have some kind of mechanical failure when we were landing after our second sortie of the day and his Harridan rolled sharply, straight into the ground, killing him instantly.

Like myself and a few of the others, Squadron Leader Pendergast wasn't officially a member of 112 Squadron, but had been co-opted out of necessity after the defeat of Cyprus. After the previous CO bought it, only a couple of weeks ago, he had taken over command of the squadron as the highest-ranking pilot. He wasn't a brilliant pilot by any means, but he knew the capabilities of his aircraft and how to use them to great effect. His awareness of what was going on around him was second to none, though, and that, more than anything else, was why he had survived so long, since the very first engagements of the war in fact - he'd flown in France, over Britain, then Greece and Cyprus, before finally ending up in Alexandria. It was also largely what had kept us from losing any pilots since he'd taken over - an equally remarkable accomplishment under the circumstances. Ironically, that record remains intact - he will never lose another pilot under his command.

Despite the fact that the field promotion to aviator lieutenant granted me by Brigadier Sir Miles Cholmondeley-Warner, the commander of the British forces in Egypt, has yet to be confirmed, it still makes me the highest ranking pilot remaining and command of the squadron now turns to me.

11 p.m.

A brief remembrance was held for Squadron Leader Pendergast this evening.

There have been too many losses in the recent months for this death to be anything out of the ordinary and indeed we have lost several men and women in the last 5 days to accidents or illness, However, the pilots of the squadron have apparently come to be seen as heroes, watching over the convoy tirelessly, keeping them safe, and the small ceremony was attended not just by the squadron and command staff, but also by most of the men and women of the convoy.

DAY 7

Alawenat, Libya.
9 p.m. 4th August 1941.

Just as it was beginning to look like we had lost ourselves in the desert, today we spotted the enemy for the first time. A flight of four Prussian MU10s - long range, twin spring fighters - appeared out of the haze to the north-east, a couple of thousand feet below us. We shadowed them for a while, taking a leaf out of their book and staying in the sun, hoping that they would turn back before they crossed the path of the convoy. Unfortunately, they didn't and when they were about to come upon the all too obvious trail marking the route, I gave the order to attack.

MU10s are notoriously difficult to down, even with cannons, which our Mk II Harridans do not have, but I managed to get a kill on our first pass by sheer weight of fire and the others got two more - testament to the experience that they had gained over the last weeks of hard fighting. The last MU10 dived away, reversing course in a sharp manoeuvre that we could not match and gaining distance over us. It was to no avail, though, as we caught up quickly and, after a couple of passes, during which we poured most of our remaining ammunition into him, we finally managed to bring him down.

I can only hope none of the pilots were able to get a signal out and report our position, although, even if they didn't, the fact that they won't be returning will tell the enemy more than enough.

As the new commanding officer, the pleasure of reporting the engagement falls to me and I went in person to Sir Miles at the main camp.

The news had, of course, preceded me.

Tempers have begun to flare in the last couple of days, due to the harsh conditions and boredom, and there have been arguments and more than a few actual fights. Worse, though, is the fact that health is starting to suffer. Sunburn and heatstroke are rife and short rations, combined with long days, are starting to take their toll. However, while the atmosphere was indeed tense, there was a new sense of urgency and purpose in the camp as each made preparations, in their own way, for a possible fight.

DAY 8

Alawenat, Libya. Near the Algerian border.
6 a.m. 5th August 1941.
I was hoping to get an early start today and takeoff just before dawn, in case the enemy should have come looking for their missing aircraft, but the weather has had other ideas.

High winds have sprung up, filling the air with sand, and visibility is down to almost zero. We could probably take off and get above the sand, but if the air didn't clear landing again would be impossible. In any case, the fitters don't want us to even touch the aircraft; there are no spare parts available and very little oil and we will begin to lose aircraft if sand were to enter anywhere vital. After what happened to Squadron Leader Pendergast, I am more than inclined to let them have their way. The vehicles are better prepared for the weather and the convoy left hours ago, but the aircraft have been covered, wrapped up tightly in canvas, and will stay that way until the weather improves, despite the fact that the enemy could even now be moving on us.

9pm.
The wind has still not let up and it is still too dangerous to fly. I have ordered the squadron to bed. We will reassess before light and if conditions are more favourable we will take off while it is still dark. We will land where the convoy stopped tonight and rewind before patrolling. It will make it a very long day for us, but it is not as if we haven't done without sleep or rest in the past.

DAY 9

Algeria. Approx. 100 miles across the border.
9 p.m. 6th August 1941.
Today, we sighted an enemy force to the east.

The weather cleared up around 4 in the morning and we took off an hour before dawn, landing at the convoy's camp site just as the world was lightening. Rewinding took very little time, as we hadn't been in the air very long, and then we took off again to take our first good look around in about a day and a half.

We hadn't even reached our patrol altitude before we spotted a large dark cloud just north of east. My first thought was it was the remnants of the storm, but I quickly realised it was too localised and could only really be one thing. I immediately ordered us to increase our height, wanting to get a better look while reducing the possibility that we would be spotted in return, but, before we could even begin climbing, my wingmate, Aerial Officer Bridget Costlington reported a sighting of bandits - four MU9s.

Puzzlingly, the enemy fighters weren't up high, scouting for us, but were low. Neither were they heading for the main convoy, which was only just visible as a distant cloud, well beyond the horizon for anything on the ground. It was Costlington again who pointed out that their course was taking them directly towards the two lorries carrying the fitters who had remained behind to make sure we took off - they must have spotted their dust cloud.

They would intercept in less than a minute, so I immediately ordered the attack.

These pilots were better, or at least more aware, than the MU10 drivers had been and when we dived on them they immediately broke into two pairs, pulling hard turns away from each other.

Costlington and I turned after one pair and I managed to get off a short burst at the leader, but I knew as soon as I fired that I had missed. Neither of the Fleas even as much as flinched as the tracer rounds flew past them - a very bad sign for us.

What followed was a fairly extended dogfight, lasting at least a few minutes - an eternity as these things go - but in the end we prevailed, with only minor damage to a couple of our machines, which was probably due more to our superior numbers as superior ability.

Afterwards, I ordered the damaged Harridans to go straight to the rendezvous point for repair and rearming and took the rest to get a better look at the enemy. Now that they knew for certain we were there, it was less important to scout unseen than it was to get an accurate picture of what we were up against so I took a calculated risk and brought our aircraft in at only six thousand feet, spaced out with a quarter of a mile between us.

We received some anti-aircraft fire, but it was disorganised as they scrambled to man and operate their guns. I didn't want to press our luck, though, and only carried out one high speed pass before swinging wide around them before reversing course towards where we had taken off from, hoping that they would assume that was where the convoy was. Only once we were out of sight did I turn us towards home.

On landing, I hastily compared notes with my pilots, then wrote up a signal for Brigadier Cholmondeley-Warner with the bad news - that the enemy force is comparable to our own, if not larger.

We went back up as soon as we were ready, but this time we went higher in order to see if there were any other enemy groups in the offing. Thankfully, it seemed that this one was the only one anywhere near. It also seemed not to have spotted our convoy yet, as it was still heading for where we'd engaged the MU9s.

We kept an eye on the enemy from a distance for the rest of the day, but they didn't deviate from their course, nor did any more fighters appear. We had very little to do, therefore, but even so, we landed more exhausted than ever because of the constant tension from the expectation that the Fleas would suddenly appear from out of the sun at any moment. I would much prefer a hard fight or three than another entire day of that.

The mood at camp when we caught up with the convoy this evening was mixed, as the fact that we are only now sighting the enemy, after making it almost three quarters of the way across the continent, has sparked conflicting emotions. It is almost unbelievable, beyond anyone's wildest expectations, that we have made it so far without challenge, but, while most have taken it in their stride as only to be expected and are resigned, yet determined, some people have taken it very hard, as their belief that we had pulled it off and that we were safe, which had been strengthening every day that the enemy didn't appear, has so abruptly and rudely proved to be only a vain hope.

Brigadier Cholmondeley-Warner has ordered the convoy to make all haste, to push the vehicles faster than before, faster than the mechanics would like us to and perhaps too fast for them to keep functioning all the way to the Atlantic.

It is a gamble - trying to outrace the Prussians, who are notoriously good at moving their pieces rapidly around the board. Personally, I think it is too much of a risk, but perhaps, hopefully, the brigadier knows something.

DAY 10

Algeria. Approx. 400 miles across the border.
8 p.m. 7th August 1941.

We lost two pilots today.

My wingmate, Aviation Sergeant Bridget Costlington, fell at the beginning of the second sortie of the day when we were jumped by twelve MU9s on our way to scout the enemy column. The youngest member of the squadron at just nineteen, she was one of only three surviving members of 112 Squadron, but that was due at least in part to the fact that there hadn't been an aircraft for her to fly for more than half of the sorties the squadron had carried out whilst based at Alexandria. However, while she may not have had the experience of the other pilots under my command, she still had more than one hundred combat sorties under her belt and was well on her way to being a very good pilot indeed.

The second casualty, during our sixth and last sortie of the day, was Aerial Officer Ranjib Qureshi, who boasted descent from members of Empress Victoria's household. He had served with Squadron Leader Pendergast in Cyprus, leading the second flight for the last year of their posting. A solid, dependable pilot, much like his mentor and friend, he had withdrawn after Pendergast's death, speaking to nobody while on the ground, but had turned into a tiger in the air - he downed five aircraft today alone. He single-handedly engaged four MU10s which were lining up a run on the convoy, preventing them from loosing even a single shot at the vehicles. He shot down two before being killed himself, but delayed them enough for me to arrive and finish the job.

Six sorties. Four during which we engaged with enemy aircraft, preventing them from overtaking and harassing the convoy. Two during which we carried out ground attacks on the enemy column.

Without any bombs for our Harridans, we cannot touch their armour, but we have succeeded in destroying at least a few of their lighter vehicles and perhaps slowed their advance slightly. It is only a matter of time before they catch up, though, even at the Brigadier's accelerated pace.

DAY 11

Near Ksabi, Algeria. Approx. 700 miles across the border.
10 p.m. 8th August 1941.

Already down to 4 aircraft after yesterday's losses, we had to fly with only 3 this morning as one of our aircraft failed the already less than stringent pre-flight tests. The fitters immediately dismantled it, laying out the pieces on the canvas of our tents and our bedrolls to protect them from the sand. They did what they could in an attempt to make it at least airworthy to fly to the next rendezvous point, but in the end there was nothing they could do and they were forced to salvage what they could and bury what they couldn't carry in their lorry (which wasn't much actually - the sight of them bouncing onto the midday airfield, with an airscrew strapped to the roof of the cab and the frame of the wings sticking out on either side, was rather amusing, apparently).

The Prussians, of course, made no allowances for our reduced numbers and, with their column so close to our convoy, they pressed forwards like sharks at the smell of blood. We are doing what we can against fearsome odds (somehow, the Prussians have managed to bring two entire squadrons of MU9s and one of MU10s this far into the desert, is there no end to their logistical brilliance?) but half a dozen MU10s got through our much reduced cordon and carried out attacks. A couple fell to anti-aircraft fire, but the rest caused quite some carnage amongst the lorries especially and many men and women lost their lives.

The cost to the squadron has been immense, though, as I was the only one to come out of the day unscathed. Aviator Sergeant Bellows nosedived into a dune as he was pursued by four MU9s and Aerial Officer Peterswill was forced to bail out after most of his wing was shot off. I'm not sure if he managed to get his glidewings open, but, even if he did, we were very close to the Prussian column and, if he is still alive, he is undoubtedly a prisoner.

That leaves two of us, myself and Aviator Sergeant Lorrensson, whose aircraft it was that failed to make it into the air. I will fly again tomorrow, but, on my own, I do not know how effective I can be, or indeed whether I will survive very long.

On the positive side, we are only 500 miles from the Atlantic coast, which we will cover in 2 days, travelling at our accelerated pace. What awaits us there, either rescue or just a trap with the sea at our backs, is anyone's guess, but it is a moot point because we won't get there unless something drastic happens; the Prussian column will overtake us before then. They may even do so tomorrow.

DAY 12

11 p.m. 9th August 1941.

With the Prussians so close, the convoy did not stop last night, even for the usual few hours of complete darkness, but continued on, the Brigadier considering that the risk of accidents, even mortal ones, was worth taking, in the face of the advancing enemy armour. I would have been left too far behind and too close to the enemy so, unfortunately, I had to follow suit, despite the much higher risk to me than to the men and women of the convoy.

The fitters had already raced on to prepare a landing strip as far ahead of the convoy as they could and I took off in darkness at 1. Navigating using dead reckoning, without any outside reference to guide me, it would have been very easy to miss the strip and I almost did - I was almost past it when a glint of firelight in the corner of my eye saved me from getting completely lost and being forced to bail out. It was about 2 in the morning when I finally landed, shaking from the near miss and feeling more exhausted than ever, and I have no memory of handing over my aircraft to the fitters or of how I got to my tent.

A packet of sealed orders we delivered for me at 4 in the morning, as the convoy was passing, but the adjutant didn't consider that she needed to bother me with them at that time because they were not to be opened until 5, my usual waking time.

In the packet, along with my orders, was a Squadron Leader's insignia with a notification of a second field promotion from the brigadier. This made me bark with laughter, surprising the adjutant, but it was either that or cry. The orders themselves were simple: I was to dual mount the spring from Sergeant Lorrensson's dismantled Harridan and take off at 5:30; I was to fly on a heading of 280° at 10,000ft until I hit the coast; if I spotted or heard nothing I was to scout the area as best I could, using as much spring tension as I felt I could spare, looking for any enemy forces that might cut us off; then fly back. All while monitoring a certain radio frequency.

After a very quick breakfast, I tuned the radio in my Harridan, then took off as ordered and headed west with the rising sun at my six.

An 800-mile round trip is at the very limit of endurance for a duel spring and I conserved tension as much as I could, flying at the Harridan's best cruising speed. After about an hour and a half I sighted the coastline in the distance and watched it slowly approaching. There were a few towns along the ocean front, but I saw nothing out of the ordinary and nothing that looked like it could possibly be my destination. I was startled, therefore, when my radio sparked to life and a distinctly English male voice asked me to identify myself. When I gave my Aleph callsign there was silence for a long while before another, different voice came on, a female one this time, which asked "Badger Five, is that you?" The voice was familiar and filled me with unexpected and extremely welcome joy - it was Dorothy Campbell, who had been in command of the air defence in Malta. After a short exchange of pleasantries she warned me, almost as an aside, to be ready for company. Even as she was doing so, a flight of Spitsteams formed up on either side of me, to my chagrin, taking me by surprise due to my being rather distracted at hearing her voice. The Spitsteams led me to a landing ground on the edge of a cliff overlooking the Atlantic and there I found a few more flights of Spitsteams, adding up to two squadrons in all, and a squadron of Harridans. I also found Dot Campbell herself. Our reunion was short, but sweet, as there was, apparently, no time to lose. I was given a spare Spitsteam to replace my beloved, but thoroughly clapped out, Harridan, and then we took to the skies en masse and I led them back to the convoy.

A battle was raging when we returned, but it was not one of the Prussians' making, it was of our own. An ambush. The only way to even the odds even slightly.

The vehicles that had moved past us at 4 were apparently only the lorries, but they had been dragging brush behind them to throw up more dust. Meanwhile the tanks and artillery had dug in, camouflaging themselves, creating a crossfire on either side of the track through some hills along which the enemy had to pass.

The battle had been raging for at least an hour when we caught sight of them and, while the British weren't outnumbered anymore, having evened the odds considerably in the first assault, they were definitely outmatched, with the Prussians having heavier armour and guns. It was only a matter of time before they were overwhelmed.

Our arrival turned the tide and, while the two squadrons took care of the MU10s that had been strafing the armour incessantly and their MU9 escorts, the Harridans, armed with bombs and cannons with armour-piercing rounds, attacked the enemy. The tide quickly turned and the majority of the enemy force was destroyed or disabled in short order. The remaining Prussians withdrew and we harassed them for as long as we could while the surviving British tanks turned and sped after the lorries.

I found out only later that the presence of the aircraft had never been assured. That messages had been exchanged with Gibraltar days before, but contact had been lost after the last long-range radio transceiver had finally given up the ghost. However, Brigadier Cholmondeley-Warner had had faith that the ships of "Taskforce G", which had stalled at Gibraltar, would be there, along with the HMS Steady and her compliment of fighters, and had ordered the attack. Not that there had been much choice in the matter; if he hadn't ambushed the Prussians then the fight would have been on the Prussians' terms and at least this way it delayed the enemy column, enabling the lorries and the majority of the personnel to escape.

I returned to the coast with the Steady's squadrons and enjoyed their hospitality at a celebratory dinner, for which I was embarrassingly the guest of honour. I felt more than a little guilty at enjoying the comfort the camp afforded when the rest of the squadron were still suffering the privations of the desert crossing, but resolved to make it up to them any way I could, starting with mentioning each and every one of them in the reports I inevitably had to compile.

DAY 13

9 a.m. 11th August 1941.

The evacuation has been completed and the ships of Taskforce G are steaming out into the Atlantic.

A second Prussian force, advancing from the north, most likely from Tangiers, was spotted by the Steady's aircraft as they flew back to the carrier, but they are still a way away and far too late. All of the vehicles, less than a quarter of those that started the trek across the desert (as well as my poor Harridan, which was far beyond salvage and not equipped for a carrier landing anyway) have been destroyed and the Prussians will find only cinders and ashes when they arrive (and quite a few rather rude messages scrawled on whatever flat surfaces could be found in the twisted remains).

I asked to be assigned to the Steady and her squadrons, but my request was refused and I have been placed on one of the ships going to Britain. I am one of the survivors, heading home to rest and recover and perhaps share our experience with the men and women there who have not seen fighting, so that, when they do, they may hopefully learn from our many mistakes.

A PILOT
LIKE ANY OTHER

AUGUST 1941

A PILOT LIKE ANY OTHER

The Empire of Japan, like the United Federation of American States, was a country at peace. Life went on as usual in Japan, just as it did in America. The people walked the streets unafraid, continuing their lives as if nothing untoward were happening in the rest of the world and industry continued unchecked, with factories, warehouses and offices unthreatened by bombs. The two countries were polar opposites, though. Everything in America was about the personal acquisition of money, while in Japan there was always a sense that everyone was working towards a common goal. The American people were also very attached to the ground, obsessed with automobiles, as they called them, some of which were even powered by gasoline. The only time they strove to reach the sky, it seemed, was by building ever taller buildings up into it. The Japanese on the other hand lived close to the ground, in touch with it and largely in harmony with it, but they took to the skies with joy in their masses on an almost daily basis.

So, while the skies of America had been relatively clear, except for a few airships and the occasional military aircraft, those of Japan were alive, the skies of the capital, Kyoto, more so.

There were a few large freight aircraft and sleek passenger aircraft high overhead, racing across the country, carrying out daily flights to the farthest reaches of Japan's islands on a schedule that was adhered to with more than military precision, but there were far more aircraft, hundreds, even thousands or them, hugging the ground, buzzing low over the towns and cities. Most kept close to the ground, only a dozen yards or so above the low rooftops, making short hops between homes or shops, but some, on longer journeys, flew higher, a couple of hundred feet above the ground, moving in ordered lines as if they were following roads in the sky. Through these moved the airship Yamato, advancing in a stately fashion, like a whale through shoals of fish, unaffected by and unconcerned with them, its enormous fans turning lazily, just fast enough to maintain steerage way as it made its way to its home.

The Yamato was the flagship of the Imperial Aerial Navy, one of several of its type, but it was also the personal transport of the emperor and the only one emblazoned with his symbol so, as the enormous beast passed overhead, the people on the ground looked up, recognised it for what it was, and immediately bowed low.

The emperor's quarters on the airship were not nearly as extensive as his quarters in his palace in Kyoto or in any of the other palaces and castles he stayed at around the country, but they were still luxurious in the extreme and fully appointed with everything he might need. There was one thing that none of those earth-bound residences contained, however - an observation lounge containing a small rock garden with a tiny *chashitsu* tea room at its centre, where the emperor could take tea or contemplate the heavens through the floor to ceiling window set at the very front of the gondola.

The emperor wasn't aboard, though, because he had sent the airship half way around the wold in secret to fetch the two women who now stood in front of those windows, gazing out at the skies of Kyoto as the imperial palace crawled closer and closer.

'That's a lot of aircraft.' Kitty murmured in wonder as her eyes roved around the sky.

'It wasn't like this when I was here in '27.' Gwen said, frowning. 'Japan didn't have an air force until they formed one for the Indochine conflict and they barely had any aircraft to speak of.' She smiled and nodded appreciatively. 'It looks like they made up for lost time, though; this is impressive, to say the least.'

Kitty leaned closer to the window, almost leaning her head against it, and squinted at one of the closest machines. Two people sat side by side inside a bubble of glass and metal, like a greatly enlarged, all-encompassing cockpit canopy. On stalks protruding from either side of its roof were mounted fans, like the ones on an airship, which tilted to guide it. It had metal legs underneath, which were shaped like an insect's and no wheels that she could discern.

'They're funny looking, though, aren't they?' she said. 'I bet they're fun! I wonder if we'll get a chance to try one out.'

Gwen chuckled and shook her head. 'Have you forgotten what we're here for?'

Kitty turned and gave her a shrug. 'Honestly? Yes. I have. We've essentially been having a luxury holiday for the last two weeks - we've eaten well, we've soaked in the bath every day,' she gave Gwen a suggestive look, 'which I could get very used to, actually... and we've slept in every morning. Well, after I got used to sleeping on the floor, I did, anyway.' She rubbed her back, which was still aching slightly, despite having had daily massages. 'At no point has anyone even mentioned the reason we've been invited to Japan.'

Gwen nodded. Kitty was right. While they had indeed been treated as honoured guests, housed in the emperor's own suite of rooms and pampered something rotten, there had been no indication whatsoever of what they would encounter when they arrived. The last and only time anyone had said anything about the prospect of an alliance between Britain and Japan was when His Imperial Majesty's Ambassador to the United Federation of American States, Hikaru Sato, had extended the invitation to them and even then he had merely stated that they were going to *discuss* it. While that might imply that it was a real possibility, it was no guarantee, and nobody had seen fit to clarify whether the alliance was favourable to the emperor or not or whether they had been invited solely because the Japanese government felt that if the Americans were at the negotiating table they should be too.

'I have a feeling we're going to have to wait for our audience with the emperor before we make any progress on that front,' Gwen said. 'And that could be days, or even weeks. Although,' she pointed out the window, 'the fact that we're going straight to the palace is probably a good sign that it won't be too long.'

The palace was apparently a no-fly area and the cloud of aircraft thinned out until suddenly the airship nosed into empty sky, granting them their first clear view of the imperial palace in all its glory. They didn't have time to fully appreciate the view, though, because the first officer of the Yamato, Commander Nakamura, one of the few people on board who spoke any English whatsoever, had appeared and was bowing to them.

Reluctantly, they turned from the window and returned the bow.

'The Yamato will dock soon,' he said, straightening, 'but it will take a while for disembarkation to be possible, so the palace is sending an *Akitsu* to collect you. It will arrive shortly.'

Kitty blinked at him. 'I'm sorry, a what?'

'An Akitsu, a "dragonfly".' The man waved at the window. 'That is what the flying machines are known as.' He motioned to the door. 'Please.'

The two pilots followed him to the door, where attendants helped the three of them to put on their shoes.

'I wonder if they'll let me fly,' Kitty said in a low voice as a *kimono*-clad woman knelt to lace up her boots, which had been polished so well she could see her face in them.

Gwen gave her a look. 'I'm sure we'll have a chance to have a go on one later, but for now, let's try not to kill ourselves before we've even spoken to His Imperial Majesty.'

The first officer smiled at them. 'The Akitsu are very easy to fly and very very safe. They have automatic gyroscopes and are designed to land gently if the controls are released. Very few have ever crashed.'

Gwen grinned at Kitty. 'Apparently even an idiot could fly one, so you might get your wish!'

When they'd first come on board the Yamato they'd been given a tour of the large gondola. They'd been shown an empty space near the emperor's quarters and told that it was the hangar. Gwen remembered thinking that it was far too small to land, or even store, an aircraft and had wondered what possible use it would be, especially with the way the aircraft that had brought them to the Yamato had docked with the gondola, hooking onto its belly. Now, though, it made perfect sense; it was just large enough to contain one of the Akitsus and one of them had already arrived, entering through a sliding door in the side of the gondola. It was one of the larger versions, with four fans and had room for up to four passengers, as well as a pilot and co-pilot. A pilot was already in place, staring fixedly forward, waiting for orders.

Gwen and Kitty climbed in, taking the two forward-facing seats at Nakamura's insistence, while he took the seat behind the empty co-pilot's chair. He sat awkwardly, with his back to the side of the aircraft, and watched the pilot nervously, almost as if he didn't trust him, as he slid them out sideways and began the descent to the ground.

The machine was very quick and they didn't have far to go, so after less than a minute they landed in the middle of a large gravel square that reminded Gwen of nothing more than a parade ground. Rank after rank of people, mostly men, but with some women and even children scattered among them, were kneeling in front of a large black and white wooden building and, as the aircraft touched down, they bent forwards and pressed their foreheads to the ground.

Nakamura seemed very relieved to be on the ground and as an attendant opened the door of the Akitsu for Gwen and Kitty, he jumped out of the other side and ran around the back of the aircraft.

Gwen smiled at him as he rejoined them. 'Are we in that much of a hurry?'

He didn't answer her, though, he just ran past them to join the front rank of the people in the square and all but threw himself to his knees.

Gwen and Kitty shared a puzzled look, but before either of them could say anything, a voice called out from behind them.

'Excuse me, Squadron Leader Stone! I believe this is yours.'

The two women turned to find that the pilot of the Akitsu had stepped out after them. He held a model biplane in his hands.

'No, I didn't...' Gwen began, but then stopped abruptly. The model was battered and worn, its green paint chipped and scratched, and it was missing a strut or two, but something about it was familiar. However, it wasn't until she looked up at the pilot and met the eyes that she had last seen staring at her from the front row of the lecture she'd given when she'd been in Kyoto for a meeting of the *Société Aéronautique* that she truly recognised it. And him. She had a sudden vision of a large room with paper walls, of straw mats with a strange smell that weren't very comfortable to sit on, and of playing with a boy who was mesmerised by the green biplane she'd just given him while her parents spoke formally with his. A boy who had been a prince, but was a man now and, on the death of his father two years ago, had become an emperor.

'Akio!' she said softly, before catching herself sharply and bowing slightly deeper than was required by protocol as an apology for her slip. 'Excuse me, I mean - Your Imperial Highness.'

She held the bow and felt Kitty copy her by her side after just a moment's hesitation.

'Please! Stand!' the young man said. He waited for them to straighten then leaned forward slightly and winked exaggeratedly, 'after all, right now, I am just your pilot. I am in disguise!'

'They let you fly one of those?' Kitty asked bluntly, pointing at the Akitsu.

'Let me?' The emperor grinned, gazing fondly at the gold and white painted machine over his shoulder. 'I don't give them the chance to refuse me! Besides, I helped design it.' He grinned, then held his hand out towards the building. 'Please.'

Without waiting for a reply, he began walking through the massed ranks of people. As he passed them, the men and women lifted from their bow and a few jumped to their feet and fell in behind him. As they followed, Gwen and Kitty soon had more than half a dozen people between them and the young emperor and they watched, still stunned by the revelation and more than a little bemused, as, without breaking his stride, the model was taken from him and he was divested of his uniform jacket. People came running from the building with folded clothing, which they held out for him and, by the time he mounted the steps he was dressed in a formal *kimono*, complete with a tall hat, fan and even swords at his hip. He paused briefly at the top of the stairs and lifted his feet to have his boots removed, but then he stepped up onto the wooden veranda that ran the length of the building and turned to face them.

Everyone in the square dropped to their knees once more and Gwen bowed, pulling a rather shell-shocked Kitty down at her side.

'We bid our British guests welcome,' the emperor declared in a voice that carried without any problem in the suddenly silent and still square, 'and we look forward to meeting with you later.'

With that, the young man turned and Gwen straightened just in time to see him disappear into the building and the wooden screens shut slowly, but firmly, behind him.

Gwen sat cross-legged at a low table, sipping green tea from a delicate cup as she watched Kitty pace back and forth.

They'd been shown to a room around the side of the building - the palace - and served tea and tiny cakes around the table by a tiny woman, who had bowed and left them immediately afterwards. Kitty had sprung up from the floor as soon as the door had slid closed and had been stalking up and down the straw mats ever since, ignoring both the tea and the view out of an open screen of a breathtakingly beautiful garden of trees, rocks, a fountain and what looked more like moss than grass. Gwen didn't blame her too much for not wanting to remain seated; even though the RAC's dress uniforms had been extensively redesigned while they'd been in Malta and the multiple layers of petticoats had been replaced with a smart and far more practical skirt, the built-in corset made sitting in an ordinary chair uncomfortable enough, let alone attempting to do it on the floor. However, Kitty's agitation wasn't as much due to any physical discomfort as it was her mental state. She had spent the last two weeks on the Yamato stewing about what had happened in America. It wasn't the various attempts on their lives that bothered her, after all it was wartime and that was an almost daily occurrence, it was the reprehensible behaviour of her country's ruling body in refusing to aid the British and signing a non-aggression pact with the Prussian aggressors. It was tantamount to treason in her eyes, a betrayal of everything she believed America stood for, and she had taken it very personally. The decision of the American senate would most likely affect her personally as well. The Yamato had maintained radio silence on its trip half way around the world so there had been no news, but she might well have been ordered home, or, in the worst possible case, declared a traitor. Kitty was desperate to get back to England, therefore, as much to be safe as to hear what was happening and she'd thought that things would be wrapped up quickly in Japan so they'd be able to hurry home. The emperor's strange behaviour had her confused and troubled, though.

Gwen put her tea down and looked up expectantly as Kitty came to a sudden halt and turned to face her.

'So? What's going on?'

Gwen looked up from her tea. 'What do you mean?'

'Well, after that welcome I thought that we were going to have the alliance signed and be on our way home by dinner, but then everything went all official and now we've been sitting around for half an hour and... and...'

The American ran out of steam and slumped to the floor on the other side of the table from Gwen. She squeaked and straightened, tugging at her tunic, probably to extract some whalebone from somewhere soft, then subsided again.

Gwen pushed a cup over to her and filled it from the pot. 'These things have to be done right,' she said, 'especially here in Japan. There is a right way to do these kinds of things, protocols to follow, bureaucratic nonsense to do to make it properly official. I doubt the emperor could rush things through, even if he wanted to.'

'But, if it wasn't a done deal, why would he fly up to get us himself?'

Gwen shrugged. 'He might just really like flying.'

Kitty grinned. 'Yes, I've heard there are some people that do.'

Gwen smiled back at her, but before they could continue speculating the door leading into the palace slid open to reveal a courtier dressed in voluminous purple and gold robes and a black hat. He bowed to them and motioned for them to follow him.

They stood awkwardly from the floor and padded after him on stockinged feet. After a surprisingly short walk they stopped at a pair of large sliding doors. The man stopped in front of them and turned to face them. Having had the correct protocol drummed into them over several very long and tedious sessions by Commander Nakamura on the Yamato, they faced him, side by side. He looked them up and down, making sure they were presentable, then grunted and turned.

The doors slid open soundlessly to reveal a wide, but not particularly deep room, lined by courtiers in the same kind of robes as their guide. They seemed to be colour coded, with blues closest to the door, then greens, reds and finally purples at the far end of the room in front of a small screen. The emperor wasn't among them and Gwen could only assume that he was behind the screen.

They followed a few steps behind the man as he walked into the room. They stopped when he stopped and bowed when he did, although not nearly as low - as foreign dignitaries it wasn't expected of them. They straightened when he did and stood calmly as he announced them in a high singsong voice. It was in Japanese so they didn't understand anything except their names, which he mangled so much that they were barely recognisable. When he finished he bowed again, only briefly this time. After a couple of seconds an answer came from beyond the screen. It was in the same singsong tones, but it was recognisably the emperor's voice. He finished after a few seconds and everyone in the room bowed this time, including Gwen and Kitty, but the man didn't straighten with them, instead he started shuffling backwards. Apparently their audience was over and Gwen and Kitty had no choice but to step backwards themselves, especially seeing as, if they didn't, the man would have bumped into them and after five steps they turned and walked out.

As soon as the doors were closed behind them they looked at the courtier, but he said nothing and just bowed and motioned for them to go back the way they had come. Kitty deflated in disappointment when she saw that they were going back to their room and trudged along, head down, scuffing her stockings on the floor. Gwen didn't show it, but she didn't feel any better; she hadn't understood what had been said, but the audience had been over for too quickly for anything to have been decided, so it had probably just been the first in a long line of meetings and audiences and official nonsense that they would have to take part in before anything important actually got done.

It seemed that they weren't staying in the room, though, because they found Commander Nakamura waiting for them on the outside terrace, along with attendants to help them with their boots. He had a brief conversation with the courtier while they sat on low wooden stools and were fussed over, then led them around the wooden walkway to the back of the palace. Once they had stepped off the walkway and onto a gravel path he slowed to let them come up beside him and gave them a wide smile.

'That went well, apparently.'

'What went well?' Kitty asked, scowling. 'Nothing happened.'

'Ah, but I assure you, a lot has happened.' He smiled at her. 'You are in Japan. Often what is not said or done is more important than what is.'

Gwen frowned. 'Alright. So, what hasn't been done, then?'

'You did not present yourselves as the uncouth and ill-mannered barbarians that some members of court have been trying to paint you as. You did not protest or try to speak out of turn when your audience ended earlier than you expected. In short, you did nothing that opponents to the idea of providing aid to Britain might use to prevent it from happening.'

'Ah.' Gwen said. 'And the emperor? Is he in favour or opposition to the idea of joining the war on Britain's side?'

Nakamura considered a moment, choosing his words carefully. 'His Imperial Highness likes and respects you, Squadron Leader, but in the end he will do what he feels is best for his people.'

'What now, then?' Kitty asked impatiently. 'Do we have to go sit around in a hotel or something and wait around for another audience? She looked around, taking in the low buildings in the distance, just visible over the walls enclosing the palace grounds. 'Does this city even have any hotels?'

'We do have such things, but they are not like the hotels that you know in Britain and America,' Nakamura said. 'However, you have been granted the honour of guest quarters here in the palace grounds. I'm taking you there now. And no, you do not have to just wait for another audience; I am not here just to guide you, but also to deliver an invitation to dinner tonight with the commander of the Imperial Japanese Air Force, his staff and the pilots of the Kyoto squadron at their base.'

Kitty's expression brightened a little. 'Well, at least we'll get to see some aircraft while we wait for the emperor to make up his mind.'

Kitty and Gwen had time for a quick wash and then, as the sun began to set, an Akitsu arrived to pick them up. It looked like the same Akitsu that had brought them from the Yamato, but it was a different pilot - they checked - and after Kitty had had her request to fly it denied again, he whisked them away to the outskirts of the city where there was a large air base. There they were welcomed personally by the commander of the Imperial Japanese Air Force, General Mitsui, who was thin, athletic, and in his late thirties or early forties - surprisingly young for such a high rank. He didn't stand on ceremony with them, introducing all and sundry or exchanging formal greetings, but just saluted them then asked them in excellent, upper-class British-accented English if they would like to inspect the squadron's aircraft before dinner.

The RAC pilots didn't need to be asked twice.

Gwen had half expected the hangars to be made of wood and paper, despite the impracticality and the fire risk that would present, but instead they found four large buildings made of iron and stone. They looked, if anything, like single storey versions of the castles that were scattered about the country, with curved gables, white painted walls and grey roofs that were decorated with statues at their ends. They were beautiful and elegant, as well as eminently functional, but they could have been made from gingerbread as far as the pilots cared because they had eyes for nothing except the aircraft lined up neatly within.

'Those aren't the aircraft we saw at the air show in Philadelphia a couple of weeks ago.' Gwen said, staring wide-eyed at the sleek green fighters.

Mitsui shrugged and gave Gwen a sympathetic look. 'We weren't going to send our best aircraft to America just to have their designs stolen.'

'Hmm,' Gwen grunted in agreement. She was still quite upset that the Americans had not only stolen the design of Excalibur, her aircraft, but had had the nerve to mass-produce it as their frontline fighter. That it was an inferior version was small comfort; they would undoubtedly work on it and steal whatever modifications she made in the future.

They came to the first of the aircraft and the general reached up to run his hand along the leading edge of its wing. 'This is the Furukawa Raijin. She first flew only two years ago, but has already proved to be very capable in a number of roles. She is almost as fast as a Spitsteam, has a very tight turning circle, which I am assured is just as good as that of an MU9, and is armed just as well as a Harridan while being just as versatile and tough.'

He smiled at them as he began to walk around the aircraft. 'Obviously, they are not as good as the aircraft of the Misfit Squadron, but we like to think they would be able to hold their own in any fight that your squadron is not a part of.'

Gwen assessed the design of the aircraft as they circled it. It was small, and a bit stubby, with a slightly more rounded nose than was conventional. Its bubble-like canopy stuck up a bit more than was usual, but was still beautifully incorporated into the smoothly clean lines of the machine and undoubtedly gave the pilot fantastic all-round vision. The wings were blunt and quite wide at the roots, which was a design choice she would never have made, but she could see how it might actually be beneficial, especially in a turn fight. All in all, it was rather conventional, reminiscent of some American designs from the late 30s, but quite a bit smaller, a lot better proportioned and far more aesthetically pleasing. It looked like it could be as good as the general claimed, but that would depend quite a lot on whether their springs were up to the job.

Gwen refused the offer of getting up onto the wing and looking into the cockpit; it wouldn't be very dignified in the skirts of the dress uniform, but the general promised that they could come back some other time to get a better look and see the aircraft in action. Kitty asked if she could have a go and he laughed, as if she were joking, but Gwen could see the hunger in her eyes and knew that she wasn't - she was missing being in the air far more than Gwen was and was starting to get a bit jittery as a result, just as she did when she couldn't get coffee for a while.

The next hangar contained twin-springed bombers, "Tanaka Takemikazuchis", that were about the same size as MU10's and bore a remarkably similar fuselage shape to the fighters, despite being from a different manufacturer. When questioned, the general just shrugged and said that they had both been designed by the same design team. He left it at that, as if it were the most normal thing in the world for manufacturers to share designers.

It was getting quite dark by then and they didn't have time to do more than walk around the first bomber they came to before they bundled into an electric vehicle, which was little more than four seats on wheels, for the short ride to the officers' mess. There, any fears and expectations of having to suffer through a long and excruciatingly formal dinner, probably seated on tatami mats with possibly only a thin cushion as a consideration to comfort, were immediately dispelled as a loud roar greeted them from the gathered pilots (both men *and* women, they were gratified to see) who immediately thrust cups into their hands.

The general took a drink himself, then turned to face them and raised his cup. 'To the Royal Aviator Corps and the heroes of the Misfit Squadron!' he shouted in English.

There was another deafening roar as the Japanese pilots tried, with wildly varying degrees of success, to repeat the toast, before silence descended as the cups were tilted to the skies.

Gwen braced herself as she lifted her own cup, fearing the bite of sake, but was pleasantly surprised to find it was beer instead, and a very tasty one at that. Her and Kitty's cups were immediately refilled, not by a steward or attendant, she was surprised to note, but by two of the pilots and she immediately lifted it. 'To the Imperial Japanese Air Force and her brave pilots!'

This time there was no effort to repeat the toast, the pilots just shouted "*kanpai*" and downed their drinks.

'Come!' The general shouted over the noise, beckoning to them. He led them through the crowded room, past a long bar that wouldn't have been out of place in the mess of any of the ranks of any of Britain's armed forces and into a dining area with a single long low table, but no chairs. The table was already laden with food and, as soon as the British had been placed at the head at the far end of the room with the general and the squadron commander, Major Tanaka, the Japanese pilots sat and immediately started grabbing what they wanted with their chopsticks.

The level of noise rose quickly as conversations started around the table and Gwen and Kitty smiled at each other; after the stiffness, formality, disappointments, danger and strain of the last few weeks this was just what they needed - a night with their own kind of people. Treaties and wars could wait for one evening.

The general was filling Gwen's cup and she picked up one of the flasks from the table to return the favour, as was customary, but froze when she caught sight of a familiar face a few yards down the table, sitting amongst the officers. The man seemed to feel her gaze on him and turned to meet her eyes. He smiled and inclined his head minutely, but then turned away and laughed at something the pilot next to him had said. She wondered if the general knew that the emperor was dressed as a pilot and laughing and joking with his men and turned to ask him, but he was holding his cup expectantly and she was obliged to apologise and fill it before doing or saying anything else unless she wanted to be rude. When she'd finished she looked at him again, but he shook his head minutely before she could say anything and instead stood fluidly and raised his cup to the room.

'His Majesty, King George!'

The men and women in the room flowed equally smoothly to their feet, but they waited for Gwen and Kitty to struggle to theirs before drinking the toast.

Cups were filled and then it was Gwen's turn again. 'His Imperial Majesty, the Emperor!'

As she drank, Gwen kept an eye on the room and the nondescript figure just down the table from her. While he didn't drink, as one would expect, none of the men and women in the room looked at him or acknowledged him in any way while they drank.

The general was letting her know, clearly, but without expressing it explicitly, that the emperor was one of them and should be treated as such while they were there.

They sat back down and the noise increased once more, with shouts and laughter resounding around the table, until it was impossible to have a conversation at a normal level.

Gwen leaned in to the general who tilted his head towards her to hear her better. 'Are your pilots usually this boisterous?'

The general laughed and shook his head. 'No! While we do have fun and find time to relax, they are usually much more serious than this.' He looked around the room, smiling fondly at the pilots before turning back to Gwen. 'They are just very excited about going to Britain,' he stated casually. 'Our orders came through an hour ago - the treaty will be signed tomorrow and we'll be moving out by the end of the week.'

Gwen stared at him, unsure as to what she had just heard and whether it was some kind of joke, but when he didn't take it back she elbowed Kitty to catch her attention.

'Kitty! Did you hear that? We're going home!'

Kitty blinked at her, then frowned and shook her head emphatically. 'No we're bloody not! I haven't flown one of those Akitsu things yet!'

TINKER TRAITOR PRINCESS SPY

AUGUST 1941

1

'Try it now, Mike!'

There was a soft hiss as steam filled the tubes supplying the engine. For a moment it seemed like nothing was happening and she was just about to tell the driver to shut down again when she became aware of a whir, increasing in pitch and volume, as the turbines started to spin.

'That got it! Cheers, darlin'!'

The young woman, barely more than a girl, in fact, shut the bonnet, pressing it down until the latch clicked. She grabbed the crate she had to stand on to reach the engines and lugged it to the side, then gave the driver a thumbs up. The driver, Mike Barnet, fancied himself a bit of a ladies' man and he gave her a cheeky wink in return and a honk of the horn before gunning the engine and roaring away. She winced at this unnecessary mistreatment of army property and watched the lorry bump out of the depot and swerve onto the road, half expecting it to falter again as yet another problem made itself known, but it didn't and she turned away, satisfied with a job well done. All the lorries at the depot were badly in need of new parts and on the point of breaking down, but tonight, at least, every single one of them would be taking their loads of food from the docks to the air raid shelters of London.

'You clocking off now, luv?' the guard, a portly soldier in his forties, called out as he closed and locked the gate behind the lorry. 'It's getting late.'

She looked up at the clock on the wall and paled; she'd lost track of time and it was now more than an hour past when she should have been on her way home. She eyed the tools she'd been using on the lorry. This was an army depot and by regulations all tools needed to be checked and oiled before being packed neatly and put back in their place in the warehouse. If she put them back out of place or in bad condition she could earn a reprimand. As a volunteer, and not an army regular, that was likely to just be slap on the wrist and a "don't do it again" rather than anything serious, but it wouldn't look good on her record when it became time to enlist.

'I'll do 'em,' the man said kindly, reading her mind, 'you just run on home - don't want your mum getting worried.'

'Thank you, Bert.' She said, stripping off her greasy protective gloves as she backed up towards the gatehouse. 'You're a life saver.'

'You can always make it up to me by bringing a couple more of those biscuits for me tea on Monday!' the man called after her.

'A whole box!' she shouted over her shoulder as she began to run.

If Bert said anything more, she didn't hear it, because the elderly woman behind the desk in the gatehouse was hard of hearing and always had the radio up as loud as it would go, drowning out even the roaring of the heavy lorries coming and going. She punched out, then waved to the woman.

'Good night, Ethel!' She shouted at the top of her voice.

The grey-haired woman looked up from her knitting and smiled, waving back and saying something in reply, but her words never made it past the music of the Jazz band playing live at the Savoy.

The street outside the depot was far emptier than it usually was, which would have told the young woman how late it was even if she hadn't seen the time, and she got to the Underground station in record time and sprinted down the steps to the platform. Thankfully, she didn't have to wait long for a train and there were even a couple of empty seats.

Nobody batted an eyelid at the state she was in. Nobody ever did. They just looked at the young woman in drab green army coveralls and cap, with splodges of oil and grease down her front and, as she could see from her reflection in the window opposite, more smeared on her face, and they saw someone who was "doing their bit". That was just as well, really, because she really didn't want them looking any closer.

A laugh from down the train to her right caught her attention and she leaned forward to see a group of men and women in Royal Navy uniforms. They were in the section of the carriage where the seats were facing forward and back rather than being down the sides and there were more than a dozen of them crowded into eight seats. They were obviously on leave and going out for the night, the war forgotten for at least a while. She smiled at their antics and watched as they joked and fooled around, but then frowned when she realised that the noise they were making just meant that the silence in the rest of the carriage was more obvious.

She looked around unobtrusively, gauging the mood, as her father had asked her to whenever she went out on her own, and wasn't happy with what she saw - gazes everywhere were downcast and there were barely any smiles in evidence except among the sailors and a couple near them, who were sitting as close as they could to each other without actually being in each other's laps.

A man in a suit to her left had his newspaper open in front of him, but it was drooping in his hands, unseen and unread, as he stared into space.

Next to him, a woman in a factory worker's coveralls sat bent over in her seat, her head in her hands, sobbing gently, ignored by all.

The boy sitting directly across from her was crying silently, a tin aircraft on his lap, the wing separated from it. He must have been all of five or six and the toy was obviously his world at that moment so he was inconsolable. His mother had her arm around him, half-heartedly trying to console him, while her own despair was plain to see on her face.

The man sitting next to the mother had empty eyes and was sipping mechanically from a hip flask that he kept putting back into his pocket only to bring it out again only moments later.

The same kinds of scenes were repeated all around her and it had been this way for the last few weeks. Ever since the news of Malta's fall and the disbanding of the Misfit Squadron had been made public, there had been very little to bring hope to the people. Quite the opposite, in fact, with all of Europe in the hands of the Prussians and their forces massing just over the channel, preparing for the invasion of the British Isles.

The war minister, Regis Cummerbund, wasn't doing anything to help the situation either.

The king had always told the truth about the war in his speeches, not keeping it from the public when things didn't go Britain's way, but he always made his listeners feel that there was yet hope, which there was, albeit less and less as time went on. The war minister on the other hand had seemingly set out to destroy morale in the country; every speech he had made since he had taken over from the king as the absolute authority over the war effort painted the situation as dire and the war as being as good as lost.

No wonder everyone was already picturing their future as a defeated nation.

Her eyes went to the floor as she sighed and began to slump down in her seat, but she caught herself, realising with a start that she had started to slip into despair herself while she should, instead, have been thinking about others.

Her eyes went to the boy in front of her and she slid off her seat and went across the carriage to crouch down in front of him. She was saddened to see the mother's arm tighten around him protectively and felt her suspicious look, but ignored her and instead focused on the boy. He didn't stop crying, but his eyes lifted to hers and there was something in them that was, if not hope, then at least curiosity.

She gave him her brightest smile. 'Is that your aircraft?'

The boy nodded slowly.

'It looks like a Spitsteam. Is that right?'

The boy nodded again and lifted the aircraft to show her. 'The wing broke. It fell and it broke.'

She nodded. 'I see. Well, you know, I've fixed quite a lot of Spitsteams. Do you think I could try to fix yours?'

There was definitely some hope in those eyes now and he nodded, quicker this time, and held the aircraft out to her without hesitation.

She took it from him carefully and inspected it. The aircraft was dented and scratched and the paint was almost gone from being played with so much. It was obviously a very well used and loved toy and it would be a shame for it to be permanently broken. There was no danger of that, though, because, as she'd thought, all that had happened was that the wing had come out of its socket because the screws holding it in place had come loose. She always carried some small tools with her and it was an easy matter to put it back together again. She tightened the other screws while she was at it, to stop it from breaking again, then gave it back.

'There we go. Good enough for an RAC pilot.'

'When I grow up I want to be a Misfit.' The boy pronounced seriously.

She nodded, equally seriously. 'Then you must learn to fix your aircraft as well as fly it. Here,' she held up the small screwdriver she'd used, 'this can be your first tool. I'll give it to you mother to keep for you and she can be your chief fitter.'

The boy beamed and looked up at his mother. 'Mummy! Did you hear that? You can be my chief fitter!'

The young woman smiled and gave the mother the screwdriver, receiving a mouthed "thank you" in return, then stood. The train was arriving at Wellington station, her stop, and when the doors slid open she stepped out, leaving the boy, who was now the centre of attention of a carriage full of smiling people, directing his mother as to how best to repair his aircraft.

Small steps.

Only a few people got out at Wellington station with her and there was nobody to see her turn her back on the arch and trot to the excessively large Rentley-Joyce autocar parked beside the entrance to Hyde Airstrip. There were two men standing next to it, one in an RAC uniform and the other in a dark suit. The man in the uniform saluted her, then melted away into the darkness while the suited man went to the back door of the vehicle.

'Evening, Godfrey. Sorry to make you wait.'

The man opened the door for her and she ducked into the vehicle.

'That's quite alright, ma'am. It's a nice night and I had pleasant company.'

It was a short ride to Buckingham Palace and, in less than ten minutes, she was in her rooms, where she stripped off her soiled coveralls and jumped into a scaldingly hot bath. Fifteen minutes later, her hair done and dressed in that evening's gown, eighteen year-old Liz Hawking, an apprentice mechanic in the Army Volunteer Reserve, who lived with her mother and younger sister in Brixton, was once again Her Royal Highness, Princess Elizabeth, the Princess of Wales, heir to the throne of the Kingdom of Great Britain, who wasn't yet sixteen.

After an unseemly rush downstairs and along several empty palace corridors, she entered a sitting room where she found King George VI and his Queen Consort, Elizabeth - her father and mother. Her eleven year-old sister, Margaret, was in the corner, playing with her current obsession, a doll's house that had belonged to great-great grandma Victoria. She had her back to the room and didn't turn around to acknowledge her.

'Good evening, father. Good evening, mother,' she greeted them formally, as her father liked, standing in front of their armchairs, not quite at attention and only slightly out of breath.

Her mother looked up briefly to give her a warm smile, but didn't stop her needlepoint. Her father placed his newspaper to the side, though, and folded his hands in his lap.

'Good evening, Elizabeth. Thank you for joining us.' His tone was stern to match the gentle reprimand for her being late, but his smile took the sting out of it.

'Sorry, father.'

'No matter,' he waved away her apology, still smiling, 'I'm sure whatever you were doing was important.'

Her father knew how many people depended on the deliveries made by the lorries she helped to keep running and he believed as she did; that her work there was far more import than a social engagement, even a royal one.

'And how are the people?' he asked.

'Things are becoming even worse, I think, father.'

'Hmm, well, I suppose we couldn't expect things to get any better without any good news to spread.'

Liz eyes slid to her father's fingers while he spoke as they, not entirely absently, tapped a small piece of paper, a telegraph slip, on the arm of his armchair.

'Is that...?'

He smiled and lifted his hand from the paper in invitation. Liz caught herself just in time before she ran to get it and instead walked calmly to her father's chair. She couldn't help read the paper as quickly as she could, though, wondering what her father was so pleased about. Her haste was for nothing, though, as she had to read it three times before she got the meaning behind the cryptic message.

She blinked, puzzled. 'Japan? Why would they throw their hat in with us?'

'Yes. I wondered that as well. So, I spoke to the Hawkings this afternoon and asked them. Apparently, Squadron Leader Stone was there with the Société Aéronautique as a child and made quite an impression on the Emperor when he was a boy.'

Liz nodded, still frowning, her mind racing to take in the implications. 'So, America has said no, but we might have an ally in Japan. The logistics of that will be difficult.'

'To say the least! Not to mention that if Japan declares for us then China will likely declare for the Prussians in response and this little war of ours will get that much bigger.' The king sighed. 'I don't like the idea of dragging more people into this conflict, but I can't say that we have much choice anymore; if we remain on our own we will lose sooner or later.'

'Can I announce this in my radio broadcast tomorrow?' Liz asked eagerly, holding up the message. 'If the people knew about it...'

She trailed off as her father shook his head.

'It is too soon. We must wait until Squadron Leader Stone manages to formalise it before making it public. If something happened and the alliance fell through, then the effect on morale would be devastating. Not to mention we would be telegraphing our intentions to the Prussians and Chinese, giving them time to prepare a response.'

He held his hand out and Liz gave the telegram one last longing look before handing it to him.

'Don't fret, Elizabeth, I'm sure we'll have some good news soon. And when we do, I promise you can be the one to announce it.' He smiled and put the slip of paper into the inside pocket of his jacket - he was wearing his Marshal of the Royal Aviator Corps uniform that night, which was rather unusual, but perhaps he was doing so to pay tribute, in the only way he could at that time, to Gwen Stone's efforts on the country's behalf. 'Now, I think we have kept our guests waiting long enough.' He tapped the arms of his chair, then stood. 'Margaret!' he called out, 'say goodnight to your dolls, please.'

While Liz's younger sister quickly went about her nightly ritual of tucking her dolls in their beds, Queen Elizabeth put her knitting away in the wooden box next to her chair then came to stand in front of Liz. She reached out to take her hands.

'You look tired, Elizabeth.'

'I'm fine, mother.'

The queen nodded and smiled gently. It was obvious she was still concerned, but she said nothing, she just reached out to smooth away an errant strand of hair from Liz's temple, then stroked her cheek before folding her hands in front of her and stepping back to stand next to her husband.

The king frowned down at Liz, as if he were seeing her properly for the first time. 'You do look tired. I hope you aren't pushing yourself too hard.'

'I'm not, father, I just had a busy day at the depot.'

'And I suppose you'll be going up to your laboratory again tonight.'

'I was hoping to, yes.'

'What are you working on at the...'

'Ready, papa!' Margaret came running over at that moment and grabbed Liz's hand.

Liz smiled at her, very glad of the interruption. She never lied to her parents and if her father had pressed she would have had to reveal how dangerous what she had planned for that night actually was. There was a real possibility that he would forbid her to do it or at least make her delay until she was more rested, which she might never be, what with how the war was going and how much she had taken upon herself.

'Thank you, Margaret!' the king said. He grinned down at her, then looked at Liz again. 'Just don't work too long, please. You know how important it is for us to put on a brave face. Especially now.'

'Yes, father. I'll get some rest, I promise.'

The king nodded in satisfaction and Liz and her sister fell in behind him as he crossed the room to the door that led towards the state rooms. They found the Marshal of the Court pacing up and down the hall outside wringing his hands, looking more worried than ever - if that was possible.

He glided over and bowed. 'Your Majesty, everything is prepared.'

Liz shared a knowing look with her father; that was the man's way of letting them know that everyone had been waiting for longer than they should have been.

The king winked at her before turning back to the marshal. 'Well, we are here now. Shall we?'

He began walking, catching the man by surprise and forcing him to run to catch up. Liz and Margaret hurried to keep up as well, while the guards who'd been standing almost unseen in the shadows of the sitting room fell into step behind them.

Ever since the attack on the palace, security had gotten much tighter. The family had moved to quarters that were closer together and easier to protect and the number of palace guards had quadrupled. As well as the six who were the family's constant companions, there were soldiers patrolling the corridors now, as well as in the gardens and courtyards. There were so many guards, in fact, that they encountered three pairs of them on the relatively short walk.

The royal party stopped outside the throne room and several attendants stepped forward to make sure the king, queen and princesses were immaculate. Liz, as always, had to stand and suffer as her hair, unruly at the best of times, but almost impossible after a day at the depot and a hasty wash, was tugged and pinned painfully beneath her tiara.

When the attendants were satisfied, they stepped back and the marshal bowed to the king before turning to the huge double doors. At his signal they were thrown open and he strode in.

'His Majesty, King George!'

The throne room was moderately full and Liz peered around discreetly as they entered and made their way to the thrones on the far side, trying to see who the guests were that night - she received a guest list before every reception she attended, but hadn't had a chance to read it that evening. She was pleased to see that the people in the room were relatively ordinary, as far as such things went. There didn't seem to be anyone that classified as a "guest of honour" who she would be forced to make small talk to for hours on end, or worse, practice some incomprehensible language with. In fact, she actually spotted a few people she wouldn't mind having very long conversations with, including a couple of scientists whose work she followed. Unfortunately, that wasn't going to be possible; she wasn't supposed to be with any one person for more than a few minutes so that she could meet as many guests as possible. For many of the guests this would be the only visit they would ever pay to the palace and her father liked them to go away at the end of the night with the memory of having spoken to royalty for at least a moment or two.

After the formal presentations, Margaret, who was too young for official duties like this, was packed off to bed and then Liz separated from her parents to mingle.

She used to enjoy evenings like these and looked forward to them. Her father wasn't snobbish and had followed the tradition started by Empress Victoria of not just inviting those people who held high office or had more money than sense, like the majority of monarchs before her or abroad. There had always been a high number of scientists, engineers and artists among the guests, who she had naturally been drawn to, but also many ordinary people holding ordinary jobs. She had quickly found that everyone, no matter their background or profession, no matter how humble, had a story to tell and she had enjoyed drawing it out of even the most shy or overawed.

Things had changed after the war minister had come to power, though, and these evenings had increasingly become more of a chore than a pleasure as Cummerbund had used his influence to get who he wanted on the guest list, including not only him, his family, his cronies in government and his various sycophants, but people he had private business with or who he was trying to butter up.

That night, the guest list wasn't all bad, because, as well as the two scientists, there was an engineer and an artist, who she enjoyed meeting, however, there were quite a large number of politicians, who she did not. Thankfully, the war minister himself wasn't there; he was odious at the best of times and was insufferable when he was playing to a crowd of supporters, but two of the ministers present were in his recently formed cabinet and they did their best to try to belittle her. They must have thought her an easy target - a pampered fifteen year-old girl who'd been hidden away from the world, but they'd underestimated her; she'd been discussing politics and current affairs with her father and tutors since she was nine and had been honing her verbal sparring skills over the last few months with the mechanics and drivers at the depot, who had no idea who she was, thought she was of age, and so hadn't spared her blushes. She gave far better than she got, therefore, and left some red and angry or embarrassed faces in her wake as she gracefully moved from one group to the next. She also got quite a bit of satisfaction thinking how much worse they would look when they found out about Gwen Stone's work in Japan - a victory that would be entirely due to the Misfit Squadron pilot and the king and that the war minister and his government wouldn't be able to take any credit for.

She'd left the two scientists until late in the reception, for after she'd spoken to the politicians, so that she could have something enjoyable to cleanse her palate with. She didn't have much time with them before dinner was announced, though, and she had to cut short an almost incomprehensible but highly enjoyable conversation on the advances the two had made together in medicinal compounds, something she knew very little about.

She bade her parents goodnight, then stood to the side as they led the procession in to the dining room, smiling and nodding to those who acknowledged her. It was all she could do to keep still as the few dozen people filed slowly past, but eventually the doors closed behind them and she spun on her heel and rushed back towards the rooms she shared with Margaret.

Her attendants helped her strip off her gown and jewellery and she dressed in a set of coveralls, wolfed down her dinner, then raced back out again.

2

The Brunel Tower was a marvel of modern engineering, which was loved and hated by Londoners in almost equal measures. It was unlike any other building in the old city and a far cry from the masterpieces of Sir Christopher Wren that had so long been the standard against which all new edifices had been judged. It was the tallest building in Britain, the tallest in Europe, in fact, and was only surpassed in height by the monstrosities they habitually built on the American continent. A glass shard that pierced the sky, during peace time it had been lit in its entirety - a beacon to guide the British home and to let them know that their monarch was there and ready to listen to their grievances. Now, with the country at war, it was dark, with blackout curtains on every window, and its summit was bristling with anti-aircraft guns. Its workshops and laboratories were busier than ever, though, with scientists and engineers of multiple disciplines working hard to find some way to help win the war, ease the suffering of the wounded, feed the hungry, or just advance their fields with equipment and generous grants provided by the king.

Liz signed in with the guards in the vaulted-roofed cathedral-like steel and glass vestibule of the building, making sure they knew that she wouldn't be coming back out the same way, then made her way to the lifts that ran up and down the very centre of the spire.

The tenth floor was entirely Liz's. Her private domain. Fixing lorries undoubtedly helped a lot of people. Thanks to the deliveries they made, thousands of people had something to eat every night as they took shelter beneath the streets of London, hiding from the bombs of the Prussian aircraft. Here, though, was where she really hoped to make a difference.

She was under no illusions that she would ever make any kind of important scientific breakthrough, or even any real advance; she lacked the necessary mathematical and theoretical knowledge and her brain wasn't wired for pure science, but that wasn't what she did here. Yes, many of the benches were taken up by experiments from all sorts of fields, but they just helped her better understand existing knowledge. Her own talents, and interests, were more practical in nature.

She'd learnt to take apart a hydrogen engine when she was nine. At ten she'd built her own steam buggy, which she'd raced around the garden until she'd crashed it into a tree and her parents had put a stop to such "indecorous behaviour". In 1937, when she was eleven, her father had told her about the "Misfit Squadron" he'd ordered formed and it had caught her imagination. She'd built her first model aircraft within a month, then, when she was twelve, had decided to construct the real thing.

Whilst drawing up the plans, she'd thought hard about how to power the aircraft. Although she was more familiar with steam engines, they were severely limiting and would require her to make sacrifices in her design, so a spring was the obvious, but boring choice. A timely article about Nikola Tesla in *The British Scientist* had given her other ideas, though, and she'd shelved her idea of producing a full size aircraft and gone back to the drawing board. She'd produced model after model powered by small batteries manufactured for her by a couple of scientists on the fifth floor in an attempt to prove the concept of an electric aircraft, but none of them came even close to taking to the air. After a very frustrating year, she was finally forced to come to the conclusion that the batteries were just too heavy and not nearly powerful enough. Reluctantly, she had given up trying to revolutionise the aviation industry, at least until battery technology improved drastically.

But then two Prussian assassins had used powered glidewings to get access to the palace in an attempt to kill her family, flying over high fences and past the guards undetected before crashing through the windows of their sitting room. It had been terrifying and they had very nearly succeeded, but, once the nightmare was over, instead of trying to block it from her mind or put it behind her, Liz had looked at the glidewings and realised that her work didn't have to go to waste.

Glidewings hadn't been designed to aid in taking lives. Quite the opposite, in fact; they had originally been developed to save lives as safety features in the first hydrogen-filled and extremely flammable Zeppelins. Early models were crude and bulky - essentially giant fixed wings made of canvas, wire and steel tubes - but they had been adapted and refined over the years as their usefulness became obvious. They were made smaller and lighter and had eventually become standard safety equipment for pilots during the first Great War.

Thanks to glidewings, a large number of British pilots survived being shot down, but too many who were shot down over the channel and forced to ditch in the sea couldn't be rescued in time. If their glidewings had been powered they could have perhaps made it back to dry land, or at least gotten closer to help. However, powered glidewings were very heavy and far too large to get into the already cramped cockpit of a fighter, or even the confines of a bomber, so a new design was clearly needed, and that was what she had been working on since the attack.

She had begun by studying the Prussian glidewings, but quickly found that they were rather crude and not nearly as elegant or efficient as British ones, so she'd discarded them and obtained a standard set of RAC glidewings to work with. Even though she had started off with a good idea of how she was going to approach the project, it still took her a month to come up with a design she was happy with and then the real work had begun. She had dismantled the glidewings and taken the thickest and strongest panels, the ones that were closest to the pilot when they deployed, down to the machine shop on the second floor. The mechanics there had cut large circular holes in the centre of the panels and she had incorporated a pair of fans, made to her exact specifications by metalworkers on the sixth floor, into them. A large and powerful, but thin and light battery, manufactured for her by the boffins on the fifth floor, had followed, attached to a simple electric motor, which bolted to the back of the case. When all was said and done, she had added perhaps thirty pounds to the weight and three and a half inches to the bulk, which wasn't at all bad for a prototype that had been cobbled together by a fifteen year-old.

She had finished last night. A proper scientist would probably have gone through days, if not weeks, of tests on the completed glidewings before carrying out a human test, but she wasn't a proper scientist and she was far too impatient, so she'd immediately put them on, then extended the wings and started the motor. She'd been delighted and not a bit surprised when the wings had lifted her off the ground; she hadn't expected them to produce nearly as much lift. However, her elation hadn't lasted very long; the wings weren't designed for hovering and she had lost control and banked violently into a nearby bench. An entire set of beakers, flasks, test tubes and condensers had been swept onto the floor and smashed before she could cut power and retract the wings.

That still counted as an extremely successful test in her book and tonight she was resolved to take the next step.

She'd left the battery charging all day and she reconnected it and bolted it back in place, then checked the electrical system. Everything was working perfectly, so she dressed in a dark grey flightsuit - a basic fabric model issued to trainee pilots that wasn't much more than a set of coveralls - put on her helmet and goggles, then strapped herself into the glidewings.

She hurried over to the windows as fast as the weight on her back would allow her and grabbed the edge of the curtains, but caught herself just in time before she pulled them open. This late in the evening it might not have been fully dark, but blackout regulations were still already in force for the night and she had just been about to turn the Brunel Tower back into a beacon, but not for her people; for whatever Fliegertruppe bombers might be on their way.

She'd broken those regulations once before, when she'd left one of her curtains half open without realising, and a sergeant major, who'd known very well who she was but hadn't cared one bit, had bawled her out for it. She'd hadn't protested, but accepted the reprimand, apologised, and promised both the soldier and herself that she wouldn't let it happen it again; after all, she was subject to the same laws as everyone else and her carelessness had put not only the people in the building at risk, but everyone in London. She'd thought that the incident would have made a sufficiently large impression on her that she wouldn't repeat her mistake, but in her eagerness to get going she almost had. It was one of her failings - she got so caught up in her work and experiments sometimes that the world around her faded away, to the extent that she often forgot to eat, missed family engagements and had once even continued working, oblivious to the fact that an air raid was under way and had to be pulled away from her workbench by one of the soldiers sent to check that everyone had evacuated.

Kicking herself, she stomped back across the room and flipped the switches on the panel on the wall, turning off not only the overhead lights, but also the ones on the benches and in the cabinets. Only then did she go and draw back the heavy velvet curtains to reveal the vast city laid out below her. She didn't take time to appreciate it as she normally would, but immediately opened one of the huge floor to ceiling windows, letting in the cool evening air. After the stuffiness of the room, made warm by so many Bunsens, batteries and electrical generators, it should have been a relief, but she didn't notice. She pulled her goggles over her eyes, tightened the straps crisscrossing her body and legs, then pressed the button to start the motor and stepped to the edge.

As a safety measure, the windows in the tower all rotated on their vertical axes, leaving large gaps. Small and simple glidewings hung on the walls next to every window so that in the event of a fire or other emergency that prevented the occupants from going down the central stairwell, they would be able to escape. The span of the RAC wings was much greater than that of the emergency glidewings, though, and they wouldn't fit through fully open, so Liz pulled the lever to the second position to only open just two of the four panels.

She performed one last check, tugging her straps and looking from side to side to make sure the wings were alright, then leaned forwards.

3

The moment when she lost her connection to the floor and gave herself over to gravity was always shocking to her, no matter how many times she carried out a glidewing jump, and her mind blanked temporarily, but she'd carried out dozens of rehearsals for just this eventuality and her body jerked into motion, almost of its own accord, carrying out the checklist she'd drummed into herself.

Left hand pull lever to fully extend wings.
Both hands to guidance straps and pull up out of dive.
Right hand to motor control and rotate knob to full power.
Visually check wings.
Both hands tighten leg straps to lift them in line with body.
Check direction of travel for obstacles.
Hands back to guidance straps and assess situation.

She was half way through the list before she'd recovered enough to not just be going through the motions and by the time she was finished, and had made sure she wasn't just going to plummet to the ground, her scientific mind was working on analysing the performance of the wings.

Existing glidewings had a backwards facing fan or propeller to create thrust that sped up the wings to give them more lift, like an aircraft. Her wings didn't work like that. Instead, the fans being embedded in the wings and facing downwards meant that they themselves provided lift.

At least that was the theory.

Spooling the fans up in a lab when the wings were stationary was vastly different from doing so during flight when the air was rushing over them and there had always been the danger that they wouldn't do anything and that the wings would just glide normally and deposit her on the ground after a short flight.

However, after only a few seconds it became patently obvious that wasn't going to be the case. In fact, the wings were actually, remarkably, and somewhat unexpectedly, carrying her higher.

Even as she reduced power to level out, a triumphant roar escaped her lips before she could stop herself. She depleted two entire lungs' worth of breath she hadn't known she'd been holding before she got herself back under control and she giggled, ashamed but at the same time amused by her outburst. It was so unlike her; so indecorous and improper, but she hadn't had anything to celebrate in such a long time and it had just slipped out. It had felt good, but once was more than enough for her and she collected herself and assessed her situation.

The window she'd chosen to jump from looked north-east over the roof of the palace, but the old building was behind her already and she was now crossing the fence and heading for the golden *Enlightenment* monument opposite the main gates. There were dozens of soldiers and guards manning barricades around the palace or patrolling the fence and grounds and dozens of faces turned up to watch her. She was relieved to see that none of the men and women were scrambling for a weapon - she had informed the captain of the guard that she would be flying that night and apparently the message had been passed along, otherwise she might have been dodging bullets at that moment.

She went over the monument depicting Empress Victoria and the dozens of engineers, scientists, philosophers, poets, artists and others who had made the *Enlightenment* possible, then orientated herself with The Mall and flew down the centre of the road, a dozen or so yards or so above the treetops. There was a group of schoolchildren hurrying towards Trafalgar Square, on their way home from a visit to the park, perhaps, and a few of them glanced up, wondering what the soldiers were looking at. They pointed and suddenly the whole group was staring up at her. They began waving, laughing and cheering, and she waved back without thinking, almost sending herself into a spin. Fortunately, though, glidewings were inherently very stable and it seemed that the fans only made them more so and she was never in any real danger of crashing or even hitting a tree. However, she increased power slightly, beginning a slight climb to take her to a safer height.

Admiralty Arch passed beneath her and, just for fun she turned towards Nelson's column. Pigeons took flight in fright from the great man's hat as she banked around him and she gave him a wink.

She knew full well that she should head straight back to the palace; a first test flight should be short, just enough to prove that things worked. It shouldn't be used to test the limits of the technology. That should come later. Much later. She was having too much fun, though, and a glance at the needle of the battery power indicator on the left guidance strap showed that she had used less than a quarter of the charge - she could afford to stay up just a little bit longer.

She gave Nelson a last smile, then pointed herself down the Strand, further away from the palace and pushed the motor a bit harder to take herself even higher. She levelled off again soon, though, not wanting to waste too much battery, and settled in to enjoy the sights and sensations of flying over her city in the early evening sky without a cockpit, cabin or gondola around her.

She gazed down at the city spread out below. It was that time of the day when people had gotten home from work, but hadn't gone out for the evening yet and the streets were almost deserted aside from the soldiers manning the barricades. It was quiet. Peaceful. Beautiful, even, looking cleaner than it ever did close up, with the sun, going down behind her, painting the buildings in hues of pink and orange and red.

Even as she had the thought, the illusion was broken, as barrage balloons lifted off from the ground across the city all around her, floating up to the end of their long cables to begin their nightly vigil. It was a stark reminder that London was a city at war and suffered nightly attacks from Prussian bombers based just over the other side of the channel on a conquered continent.

Her mood soured and it only got worse as she flew further east and came across more and more evidence of the air raids carried out by the Prussian bombers on an almost nightly basis. The destruction was greatest along the river, in the industrial areas, where whole swathes of buildings - factories, warehouses and the houses the workers lived in - had been razed to the ground, but no part of the city had been entirely spared. From this height the damage looked almost insignificant, except along the river, but she knew that thousands of lives had been lost in the year since the bombings of London and other cities had begun. Men, women, children... the bombs didn't differentiate between them, didn't care if they were involved in the war effort or not.

She would do anything to protect those people, to bring the war to a close quickly so that they would no longer be in danger, and that was why she'd taken such a risk and tested the glidewings so recklessly that night. It was Britain's pilots who would protect Britain from invasion, it was Britain's pilots who would one day lead the way to victory, and it was one of Britain's pilots who had been sent by her father to find an ally who could help stave off an invasion.

If she could save any of them, it was worth risking her own life.

The thought of Gwen Stone and what her meeting with the Emperor of Japan might mean for the future of the war lifted her spirits back up. She couldn't wait to announce the news on her radio show, to spread that hope to the people, to see the change in the faces around her when she went out, to bring back some of the indomitable will that the British had always had.

She smiled into the wind of her passage through the smoke and ether of London as she floated past St Paul's Cathedral, its dome a pinkish colour, the grime coating it, if not hidden, then at least camouflaged for a few minutes. The Tower was off to her right, about a mile away, and she was tempted to go and have a better look, but thought better of it; there were dozens of anti-aircraft gun emplacements along the river and the word that she was airborne might not have reached this far from the palace.

That sobering thought helped her decide that enough was enough for the night, that she would have plenty of chance to enjoy herself on subsequent test flights, and she was about to turn for home when movement below her caught her eye - what looked very much like one of the lorries from her depot was coming out of a side street. It was going far faster than it should and she could hear the roar of the overtaxed engine. She grinned and banked towards it, wanting to see who the driver was, but suspecting that she already knew. No wonder Mike Barnet's lorry was always breaking down if he *always* drove it like that and not just when he wanted to impress a girl. However, before she could get close enough to see the driver, a screech, followed by a loud grinding noise, came from the fan on her right and she lurched sideways. She tried to compensate, but no matter how hard she tugged on the left guidance strap she just couldn't stop the building spiral. The grinding noise was just getting worse, so she slapped her palm on the button on her chest, cutting off the motor. The reaction was immediate. The noise stopped and the wings levelled out on their own. However, even though she was no longer in any danger of slamming head first into the ground, the spin had taken her dangerously low and she was only just able to bank away from a warehouse in time to stop herself from flying face first into it. She dipped into the street the building was on, but it was only slightly wider than the wingspan of the glidewings and her wingtips scraped alarmingly along the bricks on first one side then the other, as she swerved from side to side, until she was able to line up with it properly.

With no motor she had no hope of getting back into the sky, so the only way was down and she released her legs to hang beneath her and prepared to land.

There was only one trouble with that, though; the street ended a few dozen yards away in an alleyway between two warehouses and, even though her speed was bleeding off very quickly from flying level, she was still going too fast after the sudden dive to possibly stop in time.

She dropped down as low as she could and dragged the toes of her boots along the ground. The leather scraped off in an instant to expose the protective metal toecaps underneath, but they were too smooth to provide much in the way of drag.

She wasn't about to try again with any other part of her body so there was nothing else for it - she was going to have to improvise.

She quickly took the wings up to a height from which she would be comfortable jumping to the ground, reducing her speed just a little more, and lined up with the alleyway.

She had two choices now. She could keep her wings extended and let them hit the walls on either side of the alley. They would bear the brunt of the impact, bending and quite possibly breaking beyond repair, but she would probably come out of it relatively unscathed. Or she could...

She didn't bother debating any further; there was no real choice - she wouldn't destroy an experiment that might save countless lives just to save herself from a few scratches or a broken bone at the worst.

At the very last moment, she jerked the lever to fully retract the glidewings and dropped. She hit the ground hard, just inside the alleyway, and tucked herself into a ball like her self-defence instructor had taught her. With the pack containing the wings on her back it wasn't a smooth roll by any means and she would have some lovely bruises in the morning from hitting the ground repeatedly, but it was better than sliding along the concrete on her face.

She came to a halt face down in a pile of rubble that smelled like someone had done something she really didn't want to think about in it. She rolled over and pushed her goggles, which had become smeared with something viscous and were now decidedly opaque, back onto the top of her head, then lay there, groaning, looking up into the now deep red sky through the small gap between the buildings.

'Nice landin', luv.'

Liz lifted her head and found two men watching her from a bit further up the alleyway. The one who had spoken was grinning, the fading light making his eyes gleam and his face glow red, lending him a demonic air. He was thin, a few inches taller than Liz, with greasy blond hair showing from under a flat cap and was wearing a dark brown suit and a grey shirt with a wool tie, which was a common enough outfit for the East End of London, except for the fact that the suit seemed to have been tailored and there was a thick gold pocket watch chain dangling ostentatiously from his breast pocket.

'Yeah. Very nice,' the other man growled his agreement. He was his companion's polar opposite, looming over him by at least a head and seemingly filling the alleyway with his bulk. He was dressed much the same way, but he lacked the pocket watch and his suit was made of a cheaper material and was almost comically ill-fitting, as if he'd grown out of it or hadn't been able to find one in his size. If anyone deserved the label of "henchman" it was him.

Worryingly both men had bulges in their jackets, under their armpits. Only servicemen and women were permitted to carry guns and anyone else who had them in their possession was unlikely to be up to much good.

Before she could say anything, they stepped forward and grabbed her by the arms and lifted her none too gently to her feet.

The smaller man shoved his hands deep into his pockets and rocked back and forth as he looked her up and down. 'Well, well, well, what do we have here? A damsel in distress? You're a bit out of yer way, aintcha, darlin'?'

'Yes. A bit.'

She smiled, but it was forced; she was all too familiar with the look in the man's eyes - she had seen it too often in the eyes of men who had come to the palace as guests: men who had been assessing her and her sister as prospects for marriage, despite their age; men who were used to getting their own way, no matter the cost to others; men who had destroyed others to get where they were. It was the look of a predator and she couldn't help but feel like prey at that moment. Her only hope was to try to escape quickly, before he decided what he wanted to do with her.

'Thank you for helping me. I should...' she started towards the entrance of the alleyway, but came to a halt immediately when the big man moved to block her.

'You know, it was lucky we found you first;' The thin man continued, 'there's some bad people around here,' he looked over her shoulder at the big man, 'ain't that right, Alfie?'

'Yeah, Rodney. *Bad* people.'

'So.' The man fixed his eyes on her, his wide grin still in place. 'Wotcha doin' here, luv? You in the RAC?'

'No, I'm...'

'A Flea, then? Some kinda spy?'

'No!' she protested, indignantly, 'I am *not* Prussian!'

'Then what are ya?'

'I'm a scientist. I was testing some new glidewings and...'

'Oh! A scientist!' The man interrupted, putting on a posh voice. He looked over her shoulder again. 'She's a *scientist*, Alfie.'

'Yeah, Rodney.'

The thin man laughed, then looked back to Liz. 'That's nice, that's very nice. She's gonna need a bit've 'elp, I reckon, Alfie.'

The big man chuckled. 'Yeah. *Help*, Rodney.'

'Thank you! If you could just get me to...'

'Trouble is, help *costs*, darlin'.'

The thin man took a step forwards, crowding Liz and she took an involuntary step back, but came up short when she bumped into the big man, who had advanced behind her at the same time.

'Now,' he continued, 'that glidewing've yours'll fetch a pretty penny, I reckon.' He peered over her shoulder at the pack on her back, but then he met her eyes again and his smile turned cruel. 'But you. You'd be worth...'

He lifted his hand to stroke her cheek, but before he could touch her he cried out as something struck his arm, knocking his hand away and sending him stumbling sideways.

'Is that any way to treat a lady, Rodney?'

The voice came from the imposingly large figure of a man in a long coat, silhouetted in the last of the light at the end of the alley. His right arm was extended towards them, as if he were holding a weapon.

"Oo's dat? 'Oo's dere?' The big man called out gruffly, squinting and shielding his eyes.

'Who do you think, Alfred?'

'Mr Richardson?' The big man recoiled, his face twisted in fear. He staggered back a couple of steps, narrowly missing Liz.

'We didn' mean no offence. Mr Richardson!' The thin man said urgently, picking himself up off the floor.

'None taken, now go away please.'

The figure motioned with his outstretched hand and the thin man spun on his heels and ran, his large companion lumbering after him. Only when they had disappeared around the corner at the end of the alley did he lower his arm.

'Are you well, Miss? Did those men hurt you?'

'Uh...' Liz glanced along the alley in the direction Rodney and Alfie had gone. She wasn't sure she wanted to face whoever could scare such scary men and was torn between running after them and staying. She opted to stay, reasoning that she wouldn't exactly be able to escape with the glidewings weighing her down and, anyway, at that moment she could barely stand, let alone run. 'I'm a bit bruised and battered, but otherwise I'm fine, thank you. And no, they didn't harm me.'

'Good.'

He came towards her and Liz's jaw dropped when the man was revealed to be a boy, about her age or maybe a year older, with dark eyes and greasy brown hair that was a good few inches too long. He was tall and thin, gangly in that way that some teenage boys of a certain age had. He was the complete opposite of what he'd first seemed to be, in fact; his apparent bulk supplied by about half a dozen canvas bags that hung under an overcoat that was about a dozen sizes too big for him. He wasn't holding a gun, either, but had a brass tube strapped to his forearm, which had a hose running from it that disappeared into a slit in his coat.

He stopped in front of her and looked her up and down, much as Rodney had done moments before. However, there was nothing lascivious or calculating in the boy's gaze, it was clinical, assessing. He was merely looking for information. He peered over her shoulder.

'Those are RAC glidewings. You don't look like a pilot. Did you steal them?'

'Of course not! The RAC gave them to me to experiment with.'

The boy nodded. 'That would explain it. But why? Glidewings work well enough already.'

'I've come up with a new way to make them powered,' she turned slightly to show him the pack on her back, 'without needing a bulky addition. So that a fighter pilot could carry them.'

The boy's eyes widened. 'That would save so many lives!'

'Exactly!' Liz smiled at his enthusiasm. 'Tonight was the first real test.

'Did they work?' he asked eagerly.

'Yes, for a while, but then there was a problem with one of the fans.'

The boy frowned. 'Only one?'

Liz nodded. 'Only one.'

'Hmm,' he mused, gazing into space and scratching the back of his head thoughtfully. 'That pack really isn't very big, so I'm assuming you have the fans mounted in the wings themselves. And there's no winding mechanism visible, so the motor is electrical.'

Liz stared at him. It had taken her days, if not weeks, to come up with a design concept for the glidewings and he'd worked it out in seconds, from a bare minimum of clues.

'So, the problem has to be one of two things.' The boy continued. 'Either...' He trailed off mid-sentence and looked up as air raid sirens began to squeal and searchlights stabbed into the sky above. 'Never mind, we can deal with the glidewings when we get to shelter. Come on!' He grabbed her hand and started dragging her down the alley.

She stumbled after him on legs that were decidedly unsteady after the crash landing and the encounter with the two men, but it was immediately apparent that she couldn't match his pace, even for a moment, with the glidewings weighing her down. It took only a couple of steps for the boy to realise her plight and he turned back to her.

'Here.' He flicked the quick release toggles on the straps of the glidewings and caught them as they slid down her back.

'I'll carry this for you,' he said belatedly as he easily hefted the heavy pack onto his own back and began to hurry away with it.

Liz was left with little choice but to follow him, especially seeing as she had no idea where she was or where the nearest air raid shelter was, but she would have done anyway; she found she was becoming more and more curious about this boy - there were several things about him that didn't make sense and she didn't like it when things didn't make sense.

The alley finished at a street lined with warehouses, a couple of which were bombed out, and the boy took her directly across and into another alley. They climbed over a couple of mounds of rubble, the boy practised and sure-footed, Liz not so much, and he had to turn and steady her a couple of times as she slipped and almost fell. They crossed another street, this one wider, and Liz caught sight of people at the end, hurrying in the opposite direction, but the boy took no notice and just kept going.

It was hard going, with the boy setting a punishing pace, and after only a few minutes she was starting to get quite out of breath. She was on the verge of asking for a rest when he went around the side of a factory and stopped in front of an archway with a door recessed a couple of yards into it. He looked up and down the narrow street, then stepped into the opening, motioning for her to join him. The door was completely blocked with rubble from the partially collapsed building opposite, but he inserted his hand into a gap between a brick and a smashed roofing tile and pulled. There was a click, then, with a wheeze and hiss of compressed air releasing, a large section of the rubble pivoted to the side in a single piece, leaving a gap that was just wide enough for them to squeeze through. He ushered her quickly through the door and shut it after them, leaving them in absolute darkness.

'One second, let me just...'

There was an electrical buzz and a light sprang dimly to life above them, revealing the boy standing opposite her with his hand on a lever. He smiled at her.

'Welcome to my home.'

Liz took in their surroundings and frowned. They were in a rather cramped tunnel that sloped gently downwards from the door. The ceiling was an arch of bricks with the apex only a couple of feet above them and the walls were not much wider than the door. Electric lights were suspended from the ceiling every half-dozen yards or so, but they only created small pools of light and just added to the sense of claustrophobia. The floor was concrete, with lines scored across it to provide grip.

'You live under a factory?' she asked.

The boy didn't answer, he just smiled enigmatically and started down the ramp.

After about twenty yards, the tunnel turned ninety degrees to the right, then continued to descend for another twenty or thirty yards before coming to an abrupt end at a wall of darkness. The last of the lights was a good ten feet from the opening and did nothing to illuminate whatever was beyond - it could have been a mineshaft, for all Liz could tell.

There were two large levers on the wall just before the opening and the boy smiled at her again before pulling the first one down, plunging them back into darkness.

'I don't just live here,' he said before flipping the second lever.

Lights flared beyond the tunnel's end. Unlike the ones in the tunnel, these were powerful and Liz blinked, momentarily blinded. She walked forward, tentatively at first, then more sure of herself when her eyes adjusted and she saw that she wouldn't be walking off a ledge.

She found herself on a wooden platform attached to the wall of a circular pit with a shallowly domed ceiling a few yards overhead. There was a safety rail at the front of the platform and she leant against it and looked down. The floor of the pit was about fifteen feet below her and was filled with wooden work benches, much like the ones in her laboratory.

The boy had accompanied her to the railing and she felt his eyes on her, but he looked away as soon as she turned to him and gestured down at the pit.

'This used to be an ice well. One of the biggest in London. It was abandoned about fifty years ago, but it was never filled in or anything, just locked up and forgotten about until my dad bought the factory above us. He converted it into a laboratory for himself. Now it's mine.'

'Richardson... Richardson...' she muttered to herself. 'Your father is Peter Richardson?'

'Was,' he replied quietly. 'Was Peter Richardson. He died in the very first air raid on London a year ago.'

'Oh, I'm so sorry!'

She had met Peter Richardson once, briefly, at a garden party at the palace a few years back. He had been one of a large group of scientists who were in the running for a royal grant. If she remembered correctly, he had been one of the forerunners to receive one, but had informed her father that he wouldn't accept. He had said that he was able to support his work on his own and that anything that would have been awarded to him should be given to someone who needed it.

She was truly sorry and not just for the boy's loss; for such a genius to be lost to a Prussian raid was a tragedy and a waste.

The boy shrugged. 'It's alright. I'm over it now. And it's not as if I'm the only one who's lost someone.'

There was a cargo lift to their right, but the boy moved the other way and started down a metal staircase that followed the curve of the wall.

Liz followed eagerly, peering down at the benches as she went. She was excited to get a look at the laboratory of a Newtonian Prize-winning scientist and was wondering if she'd get to see what he'd been working on when he died. However, the benches were liberally covered with what looked like scavenged junk and bits and pieces of machinery and engines in various states of disrepair. Disappointingly, there was nothing recognisable as an experiment anywhere to be seen.

The boy discarded the bags that he'd been carrying beneath his coat at the bottom of the stairs, then made a beeline for one of the few empty spots on a workbench. He put the glidewings down, grabbed some tools and started unscrewing the cover.

'What are you doing?' Liz cried, leaping down the last couple of stairs and running to his side.

'Repairing them,' he stated simply without looking up.

Her first impulse was to stop him, but something made her hold back. Whether it was the competence with which he handled his tools, his obvious thirst for knowledge, or the sudden need she was feeling to share her invention with someone who understood, she didn't know, but, whatever the reason, she quashed her protective instinct and let him continue. She pulled her helmet off her head, wrapped her goggles in it to protect them and placed it in the large pocket on her right thigh, then leaned against the bench next to him to watch

'So,' he asked as he carefully pulled the backplate off the pack containing the wings. 'What's your name?'

'Elizabeth...' she answered automatically, before she could catch herself. 'Uh, but people call me Liz.'

'Liz what?'

'Liz Hawking.' She gave him the name she was working under at the depot, the name she had chosen to honour one of her heroes, Gwen Stone, who had been Gwen Hawking until her marriage. The men and women at the depot hadn't made anything of it, but the boy looked up, taking his eyes off his work for the first time.

'Hawking? Really?' He blinked at her in surprise. 'Any relation?'

'A cousin,' she blurted out before she could stop herself. She regretted it immediately; using the name to pay tribute to Gwen was fine, but claiming kinship with her, with one of Britain's greatest heroes, was a whole other matter. At the very least it garnered interest and invited comment, which put her at risk of being caught in the lie and having her true identity revealed. If that happened she would have to give up working at the depot.

'A distant cousin,' she said, trying to fix the mistake. 'I've only met Gwen a few times and the last time was before the war. Before she became a Misfit.'

'Still, that would have been incredible. Just to get the chance to speak to her about her aircraft designs...' The boy stared into the distance for a moment, perhaps imagining how such a meeting would go, but then went back to his work. 'You'll have to get me her autograph sometime.'

'I'll see what I can do,' Liz said, knowing full well it would be highly unlikely she would ever see the boy again. 'What about you? Do I call you "Mr Richardson"?'

'Isaac.'

'Pleased to meet you, Isaac.'

The boy smiled faintly and nodded, but his full focus remained on the wings and Liz watched him carefully, ready to step in if it looked like he was going to do any permanent damage to them. She needn't have worried, though; he worked on them as expertly and familiarly as if he'd designed and built them himself.

'Electric motor. Custom battery. Fixed fans... I wonder if there would be some way to make them directional.' He muttered, more to himself than her. His deft fingers moved the fans on each side and he huffed. 'No wonder you had problems. This fan's off its bearings.'

A few turns of his screwdrivers and he'd detached the offending fan and its casing from the wing panel. It took him only a few moments more for him to completely dismantle it and he turned the fan itself over in his hands.

'Doesn't seem to be damaged, but if I were you I'd take a really close look at the blades and see if they have any tiny scratches or cracks.' He laid it to one side then turned his attention to the hub. 'Now, the Sheffield factory sent out a bad batch of ball bearings a few months ago that I've had problems with - I reckon you got some of those.'

He popped the cover off, exposing the ball bearings. Sure enough, several of them were cracked and had come to pieces, clogging the chamber and causing a cascade of problems.

'Have this sorted in a jiffy.'

The boy, Isaac, emptied the bearings into a metal tray then proceeded to clean and oil the casing. He pulled open a drawer and brought out a box of steel balls.

'These are from Leicester. No problems with these.'

The boy deftly inserted the balls into the casing, fitted the fan back in, then sealed it back up. He spun the fan around a few times by hand, making sure the action was smooth, then went about reassembling the wings.

Less than half an hour after he'd started working on them, the glidewings were back together. He clamped them down securely onto the bench, then stepped back and gestured for Liz to take over.

Liz knew that the best course of action would be to take the wings back to her own lab, dismantle them and check them over fully before testing them, but she was eager to see whether the malfunction had indeed simply been due to bad ball bearings or whether there was some deeper problem that needed resolving. She also felt that it would be ungrateful of her not to let Isaac see the results of his repair work.

She extended the wings, started the motor, then turned the knob to feed the tiniest amount of power to the fans. They turned smoothly, without making any horrid noises and she smiled, happy at the confirmation that it wasn't a design failure that had brought her down, but a mechanical one. She didn't want to press her luck, though, so she cut the power and turned off the motor.

Isaac nodded appreciatively. 'It's an elegant design and I'd love to see it in action, but you should replace the bearings on the other fan before you fly them again.'

'I will, thank you.' She folded the glidewings back into their pack. 'And thank you for saving me from those men.'

'You're welcome,' he said as he stepped forward to free the wings from their clamp.

'Who were they?' she asked.

'Rodney is the head of the Barnes family. They run all the criminal enterprises in the neighbouring territory. Alfie is his younger brother.'

'They seemed scared of you, though. And not just of your weapon.' She pointed to the tube that was still tightly strapped to his right arm. 'Pneumatic, I assume?'

Isaac raised his arm to reveal a small lever sticking out through the same hole where the hose went into his jacket. 'It is, it works with compressed air.' He pumped the lever a few times. 'It's my own design and shoots ball bearings.' He grinned. 'That bad batch is useful for something, at least.'

'You're an inventor then?' Liz asked eagerly. She enjoyed speaking to inventors just as much as she did scientists and engineers. They were jacks of all trades and tended to come up with the best ideas, even if they didn't always have the knowledge or skill to carry them out. It also explained the mess the laboratory was in and gave her hope that his father's work might be stored away somewhere and not just discarded.

He shrugged. 'I tinker around whenever I can, but most of my time is spent repairing things for my patron.' His eyes went to the bags he'd left on the floor nearby and he bit his lip nervously. 'That reminds me. I should...' He hurried over and grabbed them. They clinked and rattled as he lugged them back and lined them up on the bench in the space where the glidewings had been. 'That's who Rodney and Alfie were scared of - not me, my patron.'

'Your patron?'

'Isaac! I didn't know we were expecting guests!'

Liz spun around as a voice with an exaggeratedly upper-class accent reverberated around the room and looked up to find a middle-aged man standing on the wooden platform above them.

'Speak of the devil...' Isaac said almost inaudibly, before turning as well, rather more slowly than her. 'A friend in need, Mr Turner. I was just helping her out.'

'A friend? How delightful!'

Turner strode to the cargo lift as he spoke. He operated the controls with evident familiarity and it started down. It was extremely slow, as most cargo lifts were, and the stairs would have been much quicker, but he didn't seem to be the kind of person who would take the stairs if there was an alternative.

He smiled the whole way down, posing at the edge of the lift with one hand on his hip and the other resting on a silver-tipped walking stick, displaying himself to them. He was flamboyantly dressed in a dark green suit with purple lapels and had a fur coat draped over his shoulders, in spite of the warmth of the evening. His hair was shoulder length and curled out from under a top hat the same green as his suit, the band above its brim the purple of his lapels.

Outwardly, the man appeared harmless, a "Peacock" as her father called the men and women, largely foreign dignitaries, but not exclusively, who showed up to all types of palace functions dressed in finery and jewels. They made a lot of noise, laughing often, but said very little of real interest. They were there to see and be seen and their extravagant appearance was designed to make an essentially dull or shallow person seem more interesting.

There was more to Turner than that, though: an intentness to his gaze that didn't fit with the friendly image he was projecting; a tightness to his mouth that betrayed the fact that his wide smile wasn't quite genuine. He wasn't dressing to impress or make up for a shortfall in other areas, he was dressing to distract. He was a predator disguised as a bird of paradise, like the Misfits who painted their aircraft in outlandish colours. He reminded her of the war minister, actually, who was all smiles and smarm but had a ruthless core. This was a man to make dangerous man frightened. A man who was used to having power and wielding it against anyone who stood in his way.

After what seemed like an interminably long time, but which was probably less than a minute, the lift got to the floor and the man stepped off. His eyes never left her as he strutted towards them, tapping his cane against the floor with every stride. He stopped a few feet from her and his head tilted lightly to the side.

'Wonderful to meet you, Miss...?'

'Hawking.' She nodded politely. 'Pleased to meet you too, Mr Turner.'

He returned her, but then turned away abruptly and looked at Isaac. 'Did you find everything you need, Isaac?'

'Not everything, Mr Turner.'

'Enough to be getting on with?'

Isaac nodded and the man smiled.

'Good. Get together a list of the items you are missing and I will have someone acquire them for you.' He turned back to Liz. 'A pleasure, Miss Hawking. Don't let Isaac keep you - once he starts talking about his inventions there is no stopping him.'

He held her gaze for longer than it was comfortable, as if he were searching for something or trying to intimidate her, but she didn't flinch or look away and eventually he just spun on his heel and strode back across the workshop.

'What about the air raid?' Isaac called out. 'She can't leave until it's finished.'

Turner stepped into the lift and it began to rise. 'It is finished. The all clear sounded five minutes ago.' He looked down his nose at Liz. 'You must have been too caught up in... *things* to have heard.'

He gave them a last nod, then turned and disappeared into the darkness of the tunnel.

Liz looked to Isaac. The boy was staring down at the bags on the workbench. She was about to ask him whether he was alright, but before she could he looked up and smiled at her.

'We should get you home. Do you live far?'

'Fairly far. I came a long way on the wings. If you get me to a barricade the soldiers will be able to see me home.'

The boy considered for a second then nodded. 'Very well. There's a barricade only a few streets away.'

4

With the blackout in effect and the sun now completely down it was almost pitch black in the streets, with only the glow from the searchlights to go by. Liz didn't usually go out after dark, unless it was in one of the royal autocars, and she was feeling disconcerted by the fact that she couldn't see her way clearly, especially in such unfamiliar surroundings with so much rubble everywhere from damaged buildings. She had landed in one of the areas of London that had been hardest hit by the Prussian bombardment and there were very few buildings left completely intact. Isaac knew his way around, though, and he chose them a path that took them away from the worst hit areas and helped her over and around whatever he couldn't avoid. They had been walking for only five minutes when he suddenly stopped and pulled her into the doorway of a warehouse.

'Shh!' he hissed. 'Someone's coming.'

Liz shrank into the deepest shadows of the doorway and held as still as she could. She wondered who might be walking the streets in an industrial area at this time of night. It could be a watchman, but she doubted that would cause the concern she'd heard in Isaac's voice. Another possibility was that it was the member of a rival criminal enterprise, perhaps Rodney and Alfie coming back for some revenge. After her experiences that night, where it seemed that you couldn't walk the streets of the East End without tripping over a criminal, that seemed the most likely.

However, the man who walked past their hiding place was none of those. Dressed in a smart suit, with black dress shoes that were entirely inappropriate from the surroundings, he looked completely out of place, but was moving with a confidence that closely approximated Isaacs.

Liz only barely stifled a gasp when a searchlight beam flashed overhead. But it wasn't because it had come perilously close to banishing the darkness that was their only cover, it was because the light had revealed the pinched face, thin moustache and severely parted hair of a man she recognised.

'Come on, we'll go another way.' Isaac started to pull Liz away when the man had disappeared around a corner, but she held him back.

'Have you seen that man before?'

'Yes. He's a policeman or something. He comes around every week or so.'

'He's not a policeman,' Liz looked down the street towards where the man had gone. She was completely lost and had no idea what was in that direction, but someone like him wouldn't be caught dead in a dance hall, nightclub or pub in such a rough area and he certainly wouldn't be out on his own at night without good reason. 'I need to find out what he is doing.'

'Why? Who is he?'

Liz bit her lip. She couldn't say much without giving away. 'His name is Bantum or Banfield... Ban or Bam something, anyway. He's high up in government, so let's just say it's a matter of national security.'

Isaac gave her a sceptical look and she thought for a moment he wasn't going to help her, but then he nodded in acceptance. 'Alright, but we'll have to hurry to catch up with him.' He grinned. 'Luckily, I know a few shortcuts.'

Isaac took them through a couple of buildings, stopping to listen and look around every so often and changing directions twice. After a few minutes they entered a warehouse packed with sacks of some unidentified substance and he stopped them again and pressed a finger to his lips. The warehouse was mostly intact, except for the windows along one side, which had been blown out by a near miss and he pointed at the nearest one, then gestured for her to stay low.

Liz crept up to it in a crouch, then slowly lifted up just enough to peer out of the window.

They hadn't seen any sign of the man as they'd negotiated the deserted streets and buildings and Liz had thought they'd lost him, but there he was on the other side of the street, half-hidden in the alcove of a loading dock. He was deep in conversation with a man who was dressed in the rough clothing of an ordinary worker, but quite obviously wasn't one. His posture was completely wrong for a start; he was standing stiff and upright, like a soldier, not relaxed or slouching like the vast majority of the people she saw every day in the underground or at the depot. He was also showing no deference to the other man whatsoever, but rather treating him as an equal, which an East Ender would never do to someone so well-dressed, and especially if they knew, as she herself was certain now, that the man was one of the war minister's chief aides.

Liz stared at the second man for a few seconds, long enough to commit his face to memory, then ducked back down. 'I can't hear them. Do you have something I can make a cone with? Some cardboard or something?'

'Try one of these.' Isaac produced a small leather-covered box from a pocket and emptied the contents onto his palm.

'You have a pair of Rein's?' Liz asked, peering wide-eyed down at the extremely expensive miniature brass ear trumpets.

'Yes. Obviously.' He grinned, then gestured at the window. 'And you're missing the conversation.'

Liz worked the tiny device into her ear, then lifted her head over the windowsill again and angled the device at the men.

They were speaking urgently but softly, however, with how quiet the night was, she could still make out every word.

'... have given you everything you needed to counter, if not defeat, the Misfits at every turn! Gwen Stone is the last loose end and it's hardly our fault you failed in America!'

'We haven't failed. We will kill her and her American lover when she reappears.'

Liz shot a quick glance at Isaac, who was using the other ear trumpet to listen as well. From his shocked expression, he too had recognised the man's harsh clipped tones as being Prussian-accented English.

'No they won't.' The aide said, smiling condescendingly. 'Not unless you have agents in Japan.'

'Japan?'

'Yes!' The aide crowed. 'She's gone to Japan! Didn't know *that*, did you, old chap?'

The other man glared at him, his animosity clear. 'No. We did not. And we would appreciate any information you could bring to us about this visit.'

'Of course. And my boss would like something in return.'

'*Natürlich, Herr Bamford.* And what would the esteemed war minister like? More money? An even bigger estate in Bavaria?'

'Not this time. This time he wants reassurances. That when Britain surrenders it won't become a poor cousin of Prussia like France has. That he will be left to run the country as he sees fit, without interference, and that there will be no killings, no reprisals.'

'He already has that.'

The aide shook his head. 'He wants it in writing. Not just as a verbal promise passed on by a lackey. It must be signed and sealed by both the Kaiser and the crown prince and when the war is over it must be entered into public record both here and in Berlin.'

'I will present your demands. It will take a few days to get a reply. Shall we meet again on Sunday?'

'No can do, I'm afraid. I'm going to Scotland with the minister for a shooting weekend. Monday?'

The Prussian huffed with laughter. 'Such dedication to the war effort.'

The aide shrugged with a grin. 'If we weren't dedicated, I wouldn't be here.'

'Monday then.' The Prussian clicked the heels of his work boots together and bowed his head curtly, then the two men turned and hurried away in opposite directions.

Liz sank down and sat on the floor against the wall under the window.

Isaac slumped down beside her, looking as stunned as she felt. 'What was that?' he whispered.

Liz slowly took the ear trumpet out, then turned to him. 'That. Was treason. At the highest level.'

'Who do we tell? Obviously we can't tell the government, but who can we? The police? The army?'

Liz sat silently for a moment, considering.

'Nobody,' she said eventually. 'You're right; we can't tell anyone in government because we have no idea how deep the rot goes, but we can't go to anyone else either, because they won't believe us without proof.'

Isaac smiled wryly. 'I know I wouldn't believe us.'

Liz grinned. 'Me either.'

Her father *would* believe her, she was sure of it; his opinion of Cummerbund was as low as hers, but she couldn't tell him because he couldn't and wouldn't act without an ironclad case - to do otherwise would tear the country apart when it could least afford it.

'So,' she continued, 'there's only one thing for it: we're going to have to get proof.'

A clock rang the quarter hour somewhere nearby, perhaps from the warehouse manager's office, and Liz glanced at her chronograph. It was fifteen minutes past ten and she grimaced. 'I really should be getting home. People will be getting worried.' She looked at him, then smiled as she saw the ear trumpet in his hand. An idea sparked to life in her head and swiftly became a plan. She would need help, though - she just hoped it would be available at such short notice. 'If I come back on Monday, will you be able to get me in a position to hear their conversation?'

'I should be able to, but what will that do? Are you going to bring someone with you?'

'No, I'm going to record them. Then it won't just be someone's word against theirs.'

Isaac nodded. 'Good plan.' He stood and offered her his hand. 'Come on, then, let's get you to that barricade.'

Liz allowed him to pull her to her feet, then together they picked their way back through the building. It took them only a few minutes, padding softly along back streets and through alleys, to reach a main road, but Isaac stopped and stood against the wall before turning onto it.

'There's a barricade just around the corner, but this is as far as I go. Soldiers ask too many questions and I have too few answers.'

He held out the glidewings straps first and held them while she put them on and strapped them in place. When he finally let them go and she took their full weight she groaned; they hadn't seemed nearly as heavy a couple of hours ago.

'Thank you, Isaac.'

'You're welcome. See you Monday. I'll be in my lab all evening, so just turn up whenever you need to.'

'See you Monday.'

She gave him one last smile, then stomped heavily around the corner.

The barricade was about thirty yards away. It was a chest-high wall of sandbags that stretched from one side to the other, with smallish gaps on the pavements for pedestrians and a larger gap in the middle, currently blocked by a metal gate on wheels. It was designed to act as a checkpoint to stop the movement of contraband and, in the event of an invasion force coming up the Thames, provide a small bastion of safety. They had been thought of by some very clever men when the war first broke out, but the philosophy of war had changed considerably, as had the circumstances, and they had become obsolete. They did still provide a small command centre from which to coordinate the efforts of firefighting crews in the area, though, and were manned day and night by soldiers with radios.

She walked down the middle of the road, in clear view of the barricade, but wasn't challenged until she'd gotten within five yards of the gate.

'Halt! Who goes?' a head popped out from behind the barricade, a tin helmet sitting wonkily on it as if it had been hurriedly put on.

'Polly Wobbler,' she called out as clearly as she could.

The man laughed. 'Pull the other one, darlin'! It's got bells on!'

Another head popped up next to the first, this one wearing a helmet with three stripes on it. 'Step forward and be recognised!' this man ordered, rather more formally.

With the end of her day in sight, Liz was feeling extremely weary all of a sudden and it was hard to move with the weight on her back, but she managed to get herself walking again.

'But, sarge!' hissed the first man. 'She's havin' a laugh! You know whose codename that is?'

'Shut it, private,' the sergeant ordered firmly but quietly. 'Stand to, everyone! Open the gate.'

The gate rolled smoothly and silently to the side on its rubber wheels and the sergeant moved to stand in the middle of the gap. He stood to attention and saluted.

'Ma'am!'

Behind him, the rest of his squad - two women and the young man who had challenged her - were scrambling to form up into a line.

'Evening, sergeant. Please, stand easy.' She tried to stop in front of him, but her legs were like jelly and she stumbled. The sergeant put out an arm to help her and she grabbed it before she fell.

'Thank you.'

'Are you injured, ma'am?' he asked, concerned.

'No, no. Just tired.' She smiled at him reassuringly. 'I'm a bit lost and need some help getting home. Would you mind reporting my whereabouts and finding me a lift?'

'Of course, ma'am.'

The man half turned towards the ragged line of men and women. 'Lowe, Dunn. Get over here. Ridley, get on the blower to headquarters.' As they ran to obey his orders he turned back to Liz. 'May we help you with your gear, ma'am?'

'That would be lovely, thank you, Sergeant...?'

'Wilson, ma'am.'

'Thank you, Sergeant Wilson.'

Liz shrugged out of the glidewings and allowed the two women, Lowe and Dunn, to take it from her.

'Carefully!' the sergeant growled to them as they began to lug it away between them.

Feeling much lighter, if not really better, Liz followed them into the guard post next to the gate - a small square against the barricade, sectioned off by more sandbags where the men and women who manned the barricade could rest and store equipment.

'I know, Bill! That's what I said! But I swear...!' The private, Ridley, broke off when he saw the sergeant and Liz approaching and held the radio out to them. 'Headquarters, sarge. Ma'am.'

The sergeant took the receiver, but didn't immediately speak into it. 'I'll have this sorted out quick sharp, ma'am. Why don't you take a seat? The kettle just boiled if you'd like a cuppa.'

'Thank you, sergeant.' Liz smiled gratefully. 'That would be most welcome.'

The tea came in a white enamel mug with a chipped blue rim and the younger members of the squad stared at her while she dunked a biscuit in it. She was used to getting that kind of reaction every time she went out in public and did anything that was remotely like something a normal person would do so she didn't mind. They had no idea, of course, that she had tea every day at the depot in mugs that were in much worse state, sitting on a wooden crate in oil-stained coveralls and laughing at the often off-colour stories and jokes the men and women she worked with told. It didn't take much to put them at ease, though, just a smile and a few questions, and she found that it was much easier and far more pleasant to talk to them than it was to the majority of people that came to the palace - they weren't there to score points, they weren't analysing ever word she said for hidden meaning, or trying to work in their own agendas, they were simply passing the time while they were on duty and trying to make the most of an unexpected situation. She got them talking about themselves and found out that all three privates were eighteen and had been posted to the barricades of London for a two week stint as part of their training. They were cheerful, bright and hopeful and they firmly believed that one day soon they would get to strike the decisive blow against the Kaiser. Sergeant Wilson, on the other hand, was far more down to earth and, if not pessimistic, then at least realistic. He knew that the war wouldn't be over by Midwinter and that the fight would be harder than the youngsters expected. He was in his late fifties, had fought in the first Great War and had joined back up when the war had started, so that he could impart his knowledge and skills to the next generation. He was one of those men who was the backbone of the army and the country. He said very little to her, preferring to keep watch while his charges kept her company. 'It'll be good experience for them, ma'am, for if they ever have to babysit a VIP in the future' he'd explained, giving her a wink.

All too soon, for her at least, a black autocar pulled up in front of the barricade. It wasn't one of the huge palace autocars, but a much smaller, ordinary-looking one.

A man in a dark suit stepped out and all but marched to the gate. He nodded to Liz and showed her a warrant card. 'Willoughby, ma'am,' He said softly, 'military intelligence.'

'I'll be right with you!'

Liz put the last of her second biscuit in her mouth, washed it down with the remains of the tea, then stood. She smiled at the soldiers. 'Thank you for your hospitality, Sergeant Wilson, privates.'

The sergeant grinned. 'You're welcome, ma'am.'

He hefted her glidewings and accompanied her to the autocar. 'Safe journey home, ma'am.'

'Thank you, sergeant.'

She got in and he put the wings on the seat beside her, then closed the door. As the autocar pulled away, the squad saluted smartly and she gave them a wave before losing sight of them in the dark.

Liz sighed and relaxed back into the comfortable leather of the autocar.

'You got here quickly, Willoughby.'

'I was on duty nearby, ma'am.'

'Sorry for bringing you out so late.'

'Don't mention it, ma'am.'

The man's short answers and professional manner made it easy for Liz to lapse into silence and she closed her eyes and let the smooth motion of the vehicle and the whisper of its tyres on the road soothe her.

She didn't rest for long, though; she had a plan to put in motion and the fact that a military intelligence operative had been sent for her rather than one of the palace drivers presented her with the perfect opportunity to do so earlier than she'd expected. 'Willoughby?'

The man glanced at her in the rear-view mirror. 'Ma'am?'

'Are you on duty much longer?'

'All night, ma'am.'

'Would you do something for me, please?'

'If I can, ma'am.'

'I need to get in touch with Ophelia Flynn.'

'The Misfit Squadron pilot?'

'Yes.' Ophelia Flynn, better known as Scarlet, was the Misfit Squadron's scout, spotter and expert in covert operations. When the Misfits had been disbanded she had been assigned to the newly created "Tactical Air Squadron", which carried out sabotage and subterfuge missions on the Prussian-occupied continent. If anyone would know how to record a conversation covertly and from a safe distance it would be her. 'It's of the utmost urgency. I must speak to her this weekend.'

Willoughby frowned doubtfully. 'I'm not sure if that's possible, ma'am.'

'I know she's doing secret stuff and I don't hold any real rank, so I shouldn't be asking this, but it is a matter of national security.'

The man considered briefly, then nodded. 'I can't put you in contact with her directly, but I will get a message to her to contact you if she can.'

'That's good enough. Thank you.'

5

When Willoughby dropped Liz off at the palace the reception was still in full swing, the dinner itself only just concluding. She felt like she'd been out for most of the night, but in reality it had been less than three hours since she'd left her parents and, due to the unorthodox way she'd left her laboratory, nobody had even noticed she'd been missing.

Her father didn't seem too concerned at breakfast the next morning, either, he just looked at her over his boiled egg and soldiers when she sat down.

'Did you have a successful evening, Elizabeth?'

'Yes, thank you, father.'

'Good! Good! We shall have to invite Sir Douglas for tea and a demonstration.'

'I'll need to carry out a few more tests before I'm ready to do that.' She was, of course, planning to show her glidewings to Sir Douglas Pewtall, the commander of the Royal Aviator Corps, and certain aircraft manufacturers, such as the Hawkings, but not until she'd had a chance to inspect and repair them, then put them through their paces a bit more.

The king smiled. 'Yes, I did hear that you had to get a lift back last night. But the fact that you were on the other side of London must mean that you have at least, how do you scientists put it, proved your concept?'

She smiled back at him. 'Yes, father, you could say that.'

The king laughed, then returned his attention to the buttered strip of bread he was dipping in the runny egg. It was a guilty pleasure that he only allowed himself on the weekends and Liz watched him fondly for a moment before stifling a yawn, then applying herself to her own breakfast.

She hadn't gotten much sleep that night, with the events of the evening playing over and over in her head. She still couldn't quite believe that any British citizen would willingly provide crucial information to the enemy, let alone someone like the war minister, who was in such a high position of power, but the evidence pointed to it being true and it would certainly explain a few things - such as why the Misfits had been countered so easily and disbanded at the first opportunity. Firm evidence would be needed to convict him and remove him from office and a recording of an incriminating conversation would go a long way towards doing that. She was hoping that Scarlet could provide her with some decent recording equipment and advice on how best to use it, but if the Misfit Squadron pilot couldn't meet with her, she was going to have to find some way to get something herself. She could cobble together some kind of device easily enough and should hopefully be able to get close enough to safely use it with Isaac Richardson's help, but she was worried that she might not be able to get something of sufficient quality to stand up as evidence.

That hadn't been the only thing that had kept her awake, though - she hadn't been able to stop thinking about Isaac Richardson. How could one person, one *teenager*, be so full of contradictions? His family was wealthy - she was fairly sure the Richardsons had a manor in Devonshire - but he chose to live hidden away under a factory in war-torn London and roam the streets. His father had been very much a theoretical scientist, a creator of concepts rather than devices, but it seemed that Isaac's interests were entirely practical in nature. He spoke softly and gently, but had been more than willing to threaten violence against the two men who had accosted her. More than that, though, she also got the distinct impression that he was in some kind of trouble. Whether he was mixed up in something illegal, being coerced into something by the strange Mr Turner, or both, she didn't know. What she did know was that she wanted to help him and sincerely hoped that he would let her.

Unfortunately, there was nothing she could do about Isaac, or the war minister for that matter, for at least a couple of hours, because first she had to broadcast her weekly address to the nation.

She finished her breakfast quickly and excused herself, then made her way down to the basement, where a soundproofed recording studio had been set up by the KBC so that she and her father could make their broadcasts and announcements from the palace.

She had started making her weekly broadcast a year before, when she was fourteen. To begin with she had addressed the children of Britain and in particular those boys and girls who had been sent away from London for safety, but it had soon become apparent that just as many adults were listening in as children. Her speeches had been adjusted accordingly and, among other things, she had been tasked with giving regular updates on the battles and victories of the Misfits. It had been extremely satisfying to be able to do things like announce the victory in Muscovy or the successful defence of Gibraltar, but today, even though she was bursting to deliver the news of the pending treaty with Japan, she had to be satisfied with offering words of encouragement, urging the people to hold on and telling them that things would get better soon. It was the kind of thing she had been informed that the public liked to hear, but she couldn't help thinking that there were more important things she could say.

Her broadcasts never lasted more than ten or fifteen minutes and once the red light over the door had gone off she tidied her papers on the desk, pocketed the pen she made notes with and stood.

'That was inspiring. Almost made me cry.' A soft voice with an Irish brogue came from the shadows in the corner of the room behind her. 'But it needed some dirty jokes to really make it enjoyable. I could teach you some if you'd like?'

Liz spun around and staggered painfully back into the desk, barely managing to stifle a scream as an extremely short red-haired woman dressed in a dark grey flightsuit stepped into the pool of light surrounding the desk.

She scowled and pushed herself back upright. 'Scarlet! You scared the life out of me!'

'Sorry, Liz, but it was worth it for the look on your face!'

The Misfit pilot stood in front of Liz, her hands on her hips and grinning widely.

It was impossible to stay upset with the Irishwoman for very long, especially when she looked like she was auditioning for Peter Pan in the palace's Midwinter pantomime, and Liz smiled wryly.

'How did you get in here?'

'I have my methods.'

'Teach them to me?'

'Well, first you need a bottle of good Irish whiskey, then you need to smile at the guards like this...'

Liz laughed. 'On second thoughts, I'll let you have your secrets.'

There was a knock and one of the KBC technicians poked his head around the door.

'Your Royal Highness, are you...?' The man stopped, his jaw dropping when he saw that Liz wasn't alone.

'I'm fine, thank you. We'll be out in a moment.'

The man stared at Scarlet for a moment longer, but then remembered himself and nodded. 'Very good, ma'am.'

He retreated and the door closed behind him.

Liz looked at Scarlet. 'Shall we continue this conversation over tea?'

'Tea?' Scarlet raised an eyebrow.

'It's ten in the morning!'

Scarlet said nothing and Liz rolled her eyes. 'Very well. I will have someone bring something a little stronger to suit your preferences.'

'I knew there was a reason I got out of bed so early to come see you!'

Scarlet offered her arm and Liz took it with a chuckle and let the incorrigible woman guide her from the room.

'You want to record someone covertly?' Scarlet asked incredulously over her glass. 'Well, the equipment isn't a problem; I can go and requisition it right now and show you how to use it today, but you *do* know you're a princess, right? I mean, who do you need to eavesdrop on?'

'I...' Liz began. She still hadn't decided whether or not she should tell Scarlet about what she had overheard, but the Irishwoman took the decision out of her hands when she immediately put up her hand to cut her off.

'No, no, no! Don't tell me, don't tell me! I want to guess!' she said excitedly. 'Uh...' Her eyes alive with mischief, Scarlet looked around for inspiration. 'Someone in the palace is stealing the silverware and you want to catch them in the act. Ooo. Ooo! I bet it's that herald guy! I always thought he was a bit shifty.'

Liz couldn't help but snigger.

'No, no, that's not it, uh... You think your boyfriend is being unfaithful and you want to catch him in the act! Oops! No, that was me...' Scarlet snorted as she took a quick gulp of her drink, then went on quickly. 'Maybe... Someone is sneaking into your lab and stealing your ideas? Hmmm, possible, but unlikely; there are too many guards and you all share your ideas anyway.' She paused, frowning, turning serious all of a sudden. 'So, who, or *what*, is important enough for you of all people to need to...' She trailed off, then her eyes widened in alarm and she sat up straight in her chair. 'Oh, no. Please tell me it's not...' She looked around as if to make sure there was nobody in the room with them, even though she knew there wasn't, then leaned forward to whisper conspiratorially. 'The war minister?'

Liz gaped at her. 'How did you...?'

'Shhh!!!' Scarlet hissed waving her hand. 'Not so loud!' She stood and moved her chair, placing it right next to Liz's. 'Because he's the only man in England you and I hate more than the Kaiser or Gruber. And because there's already a file on him.'

'Really?'

'Uh huh,' the Irishwoman nodded. 'Let's just say that there are quite a few irregularities in his finances and certain business associates of his have decidedly questionable morals.'

'Oh!' Liz said.

Scarlet blinked and drew back slightly from her. 'You look surprised.' She cupped her chin in her hand and frowned at Liz. 'So, it's not embezzlement or simple corruption you're about. Which means it's worse...' Scarlet sighed. 'Alright, now you have me really bloody worried. Maybe you should tell me the whole story.'

Liz took a deep breath. 'I wasn't going to tell you, or anyone, until I had proof, but if he's already under suspicion then I suppose I don't have to worry about you not believing me.'

Scarlet grinned. 'I would have believed you anyway.'

Liz smiled, tilting her head graciously. 'Thank you.'

'You're welcome.' Scarlet refilled her glass, then knocked it back in one go. 'Ahhh! That's good stuff!' She wiped her mouth on the back of her hand, then waved the glass at Liz while she covered a burp. 'Alright, go ahead, I'm ready. And don't leave *anything* out.'

Liz chuckled and shook her head, then launched head first into her tale.

Scarlet interrupted a few times to ask questions, went white twice and refilled her glass with a shaking hand before Liz finally finished. She said nothing afterwards for almost a whole minute and Liz was starting to get anxious, thinking she might take the matter out of her hands, but then the Irishwoman laughed softly.

'Well, I've got to hand it to you, Liz! You certainly know how to stymie the Prussians. First you outwit one of their top assassins and now it looks like you're going to foil their plans for the war minister to hand Britain to them on a plate!' She laughed again, but then her expression darkened. 'That double-crossing, weak-chinned, no-good...'

Her language got steadily more colourful and Liz let her rant, taking a mental note of some of the more interesting terms and expletives that she hadn't heard before. The Irishwoman seemed to have an unending supply of them, including some that sounded quite foreign and unintelligible, and hadn't even begun to slow down almost a minute later when the door opened and Liz's personal secretary walked in, cutting her off in full flow.

'Pardon the intrusion, ma'am,' he started, after bowing shallowly, 'but you do have a full schedule today...'

'Thank you, Mr Swindon, I will be with you momentarily.'

'Very well, ma'am.' The man bowed again, then gave Scarlet a disapproving look before leaving as stiffly as he'd entered.

'He seems like a barrel of laughs,' the pilot observed sourly.

'He may not be, but thanks to him I have time for my own enjoyment and experiments instead of being mired in paperwork and appointments.' Liz stood. 'I will be finished for the day at seven. After then I will be in my laboratory in the Brunel Tower until ten. Will you be able to bring the equipment to me there?'

Scarlet finished her drink then got to her feet. Liz was only mildly surprised to see that there was no sign of unsteadiness in her, despite the bottle of Irish whiskey being half empty.

'I'll come around eight. Unless the Prussians invade before then.'

'Let's hope they don't, otherwise the war minister will never get his comeuppance.'

'I'll drink to that!' Scarlet said, snatching up the bottle and stuffing it into one of the deep thigh pockets of her flightsuit. 'Later.'

Liz chuckled as she led the way to the door. 'Do you need someone to drive you...?'

She stopped when she looked over her shoulder and found that Scarlet had disappeared. She turned in place, peering around, but there were no shadows for the woman to have melted into. Finally she gave up and shook her head in admiration. 'I should get her to show me how she does that one day...'

'It's easy!' Scarlet said, popping up from behind one of the armchairs, her grin wider than ever. 'Just find something to hide behind!'

The Irishwoman skipped over to Liz. 'However, the first lesson you need to learn is to not be so gullible!' She tapped Liz on the nose. 'And thank you for the offer, but I brought my own vehicle.'

Liz's secretary had been lurking just outside and Scarlet gave him a wink and stalked away. The palace was a maze, but somehow Scarlet knew exactly where she was going and they soon came to some French windows leading out into the garden at the back of the building.

Sitting in the middle of the lawn, watched by a squad of guards and a couple of gardeners, who looked unhappy about the state of their meticulously cared for grass, was Hummingbird, Scarlet's aircraft.

'You came in style, then.' Liz nodded appreciatively, but stopped on the patio just outside the doors, only just resisting the temptation to go to the aircraft and clamber around and over it; she didn't have time to indulge her curiosity - her duties had to come first.

'Only way to travel,' Scarlet said. 'I'll see you this evening.'

Liz nodded. 'See you this evening.'

Scarlet bounced down the steps from the patio onto the lawn and strode towards her aircraft with her hands in her pockets. She said something to the guards as she went past them, which had them laughing and nudging each other, then stopped and had a couple of words with the gardeners. Liz was pleased to see them buck up considerably, although it was a bit worrying when they looked in her direction and gave her a respectful nod and even more worrying when Scarlet turned and winked at her. The Irishwoman laughed, then ran the last few yards to Hummingbird and jumped in. The aircraft started quietly and quickly, the rotors turning ever faster, and, with a last wave to Liz, Scarlet lifted off. She banked away dangerously close to the treetops and was instantly gone.

'Ma'am?' a voice behind her prompted when she tarried just a smidgen too long.

Liz put on her best smile, then turned. 'Have someone ask what Squadron Leader Flynn promised the gardeners please, Mr Swindon, and then I am all yours.'

6

When the Prussians began bombing the cities of Britain instead of the bases of the Royal Aviator Corps, a concentrated effort was made to evacuate children to safer parts of the country. It hadn't been possible to evacuate every single child, though; there were too many and there were also parents who, understandably maybe, didn't want to be separated from their children, in spite of the risk. Those children that remained had to have their illnesses cured and their injuries, far too many of them caused by the bombs, taken care of. In London, that took place largely in the *Great Ormond Street Hospital for Children*, about a mile and a half from the palace and that was where Liz spent her morning. She was welcomed by the chief physician, who introduced her to a group of doctors and nurses - all who could be spared from duties - before taking her on a tour of the wards. She spoke to as many children as she could and exchanged a few words with their parents as well, if they were there, but the highlight of her visit came later, after a short tea break - a reading of *Peter Pan* in the largest ward.

The huge room was filled to capacity, the fifty children assigned to the ward joined by every single child who was well enough to be moved. They were sitting in chairs, on the floor and were even five or six to a bed in some places, with adults packed shoulder to shoulder against the walls and every eye was on her as she sat in the centre of them all with a book on her lap.

The hospital had quite a few copies of *Peter Pan* - the rights to the book had been donated to them by the author, J.M. Barrie - and the illustration on the front of this one showed a red-haired boy clad in leaves, smiling hugely and with his hands on his hips. It looked so uncannily like Scarlet that she couldn't help but smile.

After she had read a couple of chapters and said her goodbyes, it was back to the palace for lunch, but then she was back out again, this time far further afield, to Surrey, in fact, and one of the evacuation camps.

Not all of the children evacuated from the cities could be placed with families and instead they had to go to what were essentially boarding schools. Around a thousand children slept, ate, played and had lessons in wooden buildings that had been purposely built in wooded areas close to towns with railway stations. Teachers, who no longer had pupils in the cities, had been moved in to take care of them and continue their education and the resources that would have been allocated to their schools were instead sent to the camps. They tended to be close to the cities that the boys and girls came from and parents could come to visit on the weekends, but few did because of the unreliability of transport or the need to work.

Weekends for the children in the camps were for sport and leisure so Liz brandished a cricket bat, bowled a couple of overs and ran a couple of races before helping to serve the evening meal. She joined in, eating the same as the children and singing songs with them between courses, but then it was back in the autocar for the long ride home before it got too dark to drive safely.

They got back just before seven and after she'd said thank you to her driver and good night to Mr Swindon she rushed to her rooms to change and went straight to her laboratory.

She turned on all the lights and made her way to the bench where she'd put the glidewings, intending to work on them until Scarlet arrived, but a voice from by the windows put paid to that idea.

'Nice view from up here.'

Liz spun around and staggered painfully back into the bench, barely managing to stifle a scream as Scarlet slipped around the blackout curtains and stepped into the light.

'Not a patch on the view from Hummingbird, of course, but still nice.'

'Will you stop doing that, please?' Liz said when she'd caught her breath.

'But it's so much fun!'

Liz gave her a scathing look. 'Is it?'

'It is for me, anyway.'

Scarlet laughed then picked up a canvas bag from the floor and dumped it onto the nearest workbench. Liz winced when she saw that the equipment on it, some of it quite sensitive and delicate, had already been pushed aside or piled up haphazardly to make room.

'Here you go. This should get the job done.'

Scarlet started unpacking the bag, laying its contents out neatly, with far more care than she'd moved Liz's delicate instruments. Once she was done she tossed the bag onto the floor, then gestured to the first item.

'From what you described to me, it didn't sound like you were going to be able to prepare the way and install any microphones beforehand, so I've gotten you a directional microphone.' She patted a conical device, about six inches long, with a long thick wire coming from its narrow end. 'Best range for this is eight to ten yards. Further than that and the voices will become indistinct and you'll be picking up too much ambient sound. Closer and you'll have to keep moving it back and forth to point at whoever is speaking at the time, unless they're in kissing distance. Which I assume they won't be.' She grinned, but went straight on without waiting for an answer. She picked up a box, about a foot square and six inches thick. 'This is the recorder. It's spring powered and wound using the handle on the side. It takes standard spools of magnetic tape, of which I've brought two. They can record up to thirty minutes each, so that should easily be enough for one conversation.' She showed Liz the round spools of tape, then picked up the small brass tin that was next to them. 'These are earphones, so you can listen in - they plug into the small hole on the side next to the hole for the lead from the microphone.' She lined everything up again, then demonstrated preparing the recording device, attaching the microphone, loading one of the tapes and clipping the earphones over her ears. She then extended the telescopic pole the microphone was mounted on and pointed it across the room. 'Once everything is in place you turn it on with this button and record and pause using these buttons. When you're finished press the stop button and then this little red button here will cut the tape and eject the recorded portion of it out of the side, tightly wound, sealed in wax paper and ready to go on a pigeon's leg, swallowed, or hidden somewhere unmentionable.'

Scarlet laughed as Liz screwed up her face in distaste. 'If all a spy had to worry about was where to hide a tiny wax packet, they'd be more than happy, believe me!'

She unplugged everything and took out the spool of tape, then stood back and motioned to the recorder. 'Your turn.'

For the next five minutes Scarlet had Liz putting together the equipment, pointing the microphone at her as she whispered from across the room, pretending to make a recording, then taking it apart again. She then made her do it in the dark for a few minutes more. When she was satisfied she showed Liz how to pack the equipment into a green metal case which would protect it.

'Last thing I've got for you is this.' She reached down to the bag on the floor and pulled out a garment that looked like a cross between coveralls and a flightsuit.

'I requisitioned this for you from stores. It has one of those long names that scientists with more brains than sense like to give things, but we just call it a "sneak suit". We wear them on missions to blend into most backgrounds and become essentially invisible at night. It has more pockets than you can ever need and places to attach equipment, like the case for the recording device. I've already stocked it with a few supplies for you, so I suggest you put it on sometime and have a good root around! It's yours to keep, by the way; if you plan to go gallivanting around London at night then you should be a bit better prepared.'

Liz took the dark grey suit. It was made of a material that felt rough, like canvas, but was still flexible and there were so many pockets it almost looked like it was made of them. 'Thank you. This will really come in handy.'

Scarlet smiled. 'Anything I can do to keep you safe. Speaking of which - I'm supposed to be going on a mission tomorrow for a few days,' she tapped her nose, 'don't tell anyone! But I can hand it off to someone else and go with you if you want.'

Liz was very tempted to accept the offer. She was loath to admit it, but she was scared to go back to the East End of London at night, scared that she might run afoul of the denizens again and that nobody would be there to rescue her this time. She also knew that Scarlet would do a much better job of getting what they needed to oust the war minister. However, if she turned up with someone else it might scare Isaac off and she couldn't risk that. She also had to admit there was something about him that appealed to her and she really wanted to be alone with him so that she could find out more about him.

'I think it would be best if I went on my own. We don't know who is on the war minister's payroll or sympathetic to him, so the fewer people who know something is going on the better. Besides, Isaac knows his way around better than anyone. He can take care of me.'

Scarlet frowned. 'I'm not sure I'm comfortable putting your life in the hands of a boy with no training, but alright. I've put a radio in the big pocket on the side of the right thigh. It's already tuned to the emergency frequency. At the first sign of things going pear-shaped you give your codename and location and people will come running from all over.'

'That's good to know. Thank you.'

Scarlet nodded, but then stood there staring at Liz. After a while she shook her head and looked away. She sighed. 'I don't like this. Just take care, alright? And don't do anything stupid.'

'You mean, don't act like a Misfit?'

Scarlet snorted. 'Exactly.'

7

Sunday was Liz's own, apart from meals with her family, and she spent most of it in her laboratory, doing everything she could to make sure she was ready for Monday evening. She practised a few more times with the recording device and loaded up the "sneak suit" with any and all provisions she thought she might need, although that wasn't much seeing as Scarlet had already left her with a fairly comprehensive set of surveillance and survival tools in the pockets, but she spent most of the day working on the glidewings.

The glidewings were essential to her plan. She'd considered using some other, more conventional, method of getting to Isaac's workshop, but in the end she'd decided to leave the palace under cover of another test. There would be less questions that way, less need to rely on anyone else for transport and less possibility that anyone would be able to follow her. If she was going to do that, she couldn't afford a repeat of the accident, so she dismantled them and checked everything. She replaced the ball bearings as Isaac had recommended, then inspected the fan on the side that had broken. She found that three of the blades had minor damage to them and one had a large crack. She'd had the machine shop make her a dozen blades more than she'd needed as spares, though, so it was a simple matter to swap them out. After that, she made sure that the wiring hadn't come loose and soldered a couple of contacts that she wasn't sure about, then tested the battery, which she had made sure was fully charged.

It was very late on Sunday night when she finally put the wings back together again and she went to bed extremely tired, but satisfied that she was as ready as she could be for whatever the next evening would bring.

She went to work at the depot early on Monday morning, taking Bert a packet of biscuits, stolen from the palace pantry, as she'd promised, and threw herself into her work, knowing that the time would pass much quicker if she kept herself busy.

Before she knew it the evening had rolled around. Now that the time to act was upon her she didn't hesitate or allow herself to doubt, she just dressed in the sneak suit, clipped the recorder to side of her leg, put on the glidewings, then ran full tilt at the window and leapt into the evening. She immediately extended the wings to their full extent and powered up the motor to full so that she didn't lose too much altitude while she was gathering speed. She kept it at full power for almost a minute longer, gaining more height so that she would just be a grey dot against the grey clouds and not nearly as visible to the pedestrians and soldiers in the streets as she had been during her first flight. That flight had been exhilarating. So close to the ground, the sensation had been that it was rushing past her, like racing through the countryside on horseback. Flying so much higher she had time to take in the scenery, like she was on a leisurely drive.

She'd pinpointed the location of Isaac's building on a map, but with the failing light and so much of the area in ruins it took her a few minutes of circling before she was sure she knew which one it was and it took her a few minutes more to find a place that was open enough, but still moderately concealed, where she could safely land. She settled on a street a couple of blocks over from her destination that was wide enough for her wings and circled it a couple of times to make sure it was as clear of obstructions and pitfalls as it seemed. While she did so it occurred to her that this was her last chance to reconsider, to fly back home and get the proof some other way; once she landed she wouldn't be able to get back off the ground and summoning help from a barricade in the same area twice might raise a few flags and most likely alert her quarry.

She banished the idea from her mind almost as soon as it appeared, then turned the motor down and began her descent.

Her landing in the East End of London was rather smoother this time, but still not nearly perfect. She had hundreds of glidewing landings under her belt, both because anyone with a lab in the Brunel Tower was given basic training in their use in case of emergencies and because of her long-time interest in flight. However, the added weight of the motor threw her balance off and increased the stall speed of the wings so that, instead of being able to rid herself of her forward momentum in just a few steps, she ended up running a twenty-yard dash, stumbling over loose cobbles and nearly falling on her face at least twice, before she could come to a halt.

She shut down the motor and retracted the glidewings, then ran into a nearby doorway and concealed herself in the shadows as best she could, fighting to calm her breathing and her racing heart as she watched and waited to see if her arrival had attracted any interest. After a few minutes, when she was sure that nobody was coming and she had her body under control she slipped out and hurried down the street.

She found Isaac's hidden entrance easily enough and again made sure nobody was watching before reaching into the rubble and pulling the lever to let herself in. The tunnel was dark, but she didn't bother turning the lights on, she just wound up the small torch she'd found in the suit and padded silently down the slope in the soft-soled shoes that had also come with it.

The lights were on in the laboratory at the end of the tunnel and Liz went up to the rail and looked down into the pit. Isaac was at a bench to the left, near the bottom of the stairs. He was so engrossed in his work that he didn't seem to notice her come in and didn't look up, so she leaned against the rail and settled in to watch, curious as to what he was doing, but also not wanting to disturb him while he was busy. He was tugging wires, as if they were weeds, out of a small cylindrical brass casing that was hinged open down the middle, inspecting them by running them through his hands, discarding some by throwing them to the floor at his feet and keeping others. The wires were followed shortly after by an assortment of electrical and mechanical components. These he treated with more care, cleaning them and placing them carefully to one side. The casing got his full attention next. He picked it up and tilted it back and forth as he peered inside, putting his face right up to it so that his nose was almost touching it, as if he were smelling it. A wire brush appeared as if from nowhere and he scrubbed inside for a few moments, then produced a hammer and started tapping at something.

Liz's vantage point wasn't ideal; she was too far away to see precisely what he was doing and his head kept getting in the way anyway, so she turned and started tiptoeing down the stairs, wanting to get into a better position before he started reassembling whatever it was he was working on.

The weight of the glidewings made sneaking around a tricky prospect, though, and Isaac jumped as her footsteps resounded on the wooden stairs. He spun around and blinked up at her in surprise.

'What are you doing here?' he asked, then frowned. 'Don't tell me it's Monday already.'

'I'm afraid so.'

'Drat!' the boy said.

'Drat?'

'Oh, sorry, not drat because you're here, drat because I was supposed to have finished all this,' he waved vaguely at the workbench behind him, 'by Sunday.'

He peered at her with his head on one side, looking her up and down as she came down the last few stairs. There was nothing in his gaze except for clinical inspection; he was merely examining the suit Scarlet had given her, but Liz could still feel her cheeks heat up. The sneak suit wasn't tight, but it also wasn't nearly as shapeless as coveralls and revealed more about her figure than she was comfortable with.

She turned away to cover her embarrassment and slipped the glidewings off her shoulders. She put them on the floor at the base of the stairs, then moved quickly to his side and looked at the brass casing on the workbench. 'What are you working on?'

'You tell me.' He said, grinning.

She returned his grin, accepting the challenge.

She examined the casing, grunting as she saw the heating element and the clockwork mechanism that powered it. She didn't really need to look at the components laid out next to the casing to know what it was, but she did anyway, not wanting any surprises. There weren't any and she shrugged.

'Too easy. Or should I say *teasy*.'

'Teasy?' Isaac frowned, puzzled. 'What does that mean?'

'*Tea*-sy? Because it's a tea urn?' Liz sighed at the boy's blank face; the men and women at the depot would have lapped that one up. 'Never mind.'

Isaac stared at her a second more, then just looked down at the urn. 'It was dropped a few too many times and tea had gotten into the mechanism. All I had to do was clean it up and replace a few of the wires. Once it's put back together and sealed up properly it'll be ready to go.'

'Is this what you do for Mr Turner?'

He nodded. 'It's mostly small stuff like this, kitchen appliances and such, but occasionally I get bigger things.' He jerked his chin in the direction of a steam engine on a trolley shoved up against the wall. 'And then there's...'

The boy's eyes went towards a bench across the room, but then he stopped talking abruptly and gave her a nervous look.

'Then there's what?' she asked.

He shook his head. 'Nothing. Just... Other things.' He turned away and bent over the urn and began putting the components back in, studiously avoiding her gaze.

He wasn't looking at her, so Liz snuck a glance across the room at the bench. She couldn't tell what was on it because it was covered with a tarpaulin, but undoubtedly it was part of the trouble she'd sensed. She didn't press him about it, though, much as she would have liked to, she just stood silently and watched him work.

After a minute he paused in what he was doing and looked up. 'What's the time?'

Liz glanced at her chronograph. 'A few minutes to eight.'

He grunted. 'We have about an hour before we have to leave, then.' He gestured at the mess on the bench and the one next to it. 'Grab some tools, find something you recognise, and let's see what you can do.'

Liz cobbled together parts from three smashed phonographs to make one good one, replaced a couple of transistors in an imported *Edisound* radio and made a start on dismantling the engine, but then it was time to go and they placed the repaired items onto the cargo lift, then stood together at the large sink under the stairs to wash up.

They had barely spoken while they'd been working, but Liz didn't see it as a missed opportunity or wasted time. Isaac wasn't like the politicians and dignitaries she met at the palace, who needed to fill a silence with inane small talk, nor was he like the people she worked with at the depot, who were readily accepting of a new face, especially one who was useful. He struck her as being more like some of the children she'd met, especially at the hospital, who had seen more than they should have, who were suspicious of everyone and who you just sat with until they got comfortable enough to open up.

He wasn't won over, by any means, but his manner wasn't as stiff and formal and the smile, when he handed her a towel, almost reached his eyes.

'I've been a bit distracted lately and gotten behind on my work,' he said hesitantly, 'but thanks to you I'm not as far behind as I would have been.'

'Distracted?'

He nodded, but didn't elaborate so she went on. 'You're helping me and I'm glad that I could do something to help you in return.'

She handed him back the towel, then let Isaac help her strap the glidewings back on. She'd considered leaving them behind, as much as to have an excuse to come back and spend more time with Isaac as to not carry them, but had discarded the idea - if the men started their meeting late, or went on longer than expected, she needed to be able to go straight back to the palace before the alarm was raised and, besides, she was getting used to the weight now and it wasn't so much of a hardship.

They climbed the stairs and Isaac was just about to turn off the lights when a voice floated down the tunnel to them.

'Off out, Isaac?'

Liz recognised Mr Turner by his over-the-top accent and the tapping of his cane even before he appeared in all his glory from out of the darkness. He stopped in the mouth of the tunnel, blocking their way.

'Work done?'

'Yes, Mr Turner.'

'Already?'

'Yes, Mr Turner.'

'And now you have enough time to go promenading with your friend. Maybe I should bring more for you to do. Hmm?'

Isaac hung his head like a child being scolded. 'Yes, Mr Turner.'

'Well, don't let me keep you. I'm sure the boys can manage everything without you.'

He moved to the side and two large men stepped into the light. They brushed by Isaac and Liz and clomped down the stairs.

Isaac barely waited for the way to be clear before grabbing Liz's hand and pulling her towards the tunnel.

'Good night, Miss Hawking.' Turner touched the head of his cane to his temple in salute and grinned at Liz as she went past. 'Lovely to see you again.'

'Good night, Mr Turner.' Liz nodded to him, keeping her manners impeccable and her intense dislike of him for his falseness and the way he treated Isaac out of her expression.

The boy held Liz's hand all the way up the tunnel, but when they got out into the street he seemed to realise what he was doing and let her go, his face turning red.

'Sorry.'

Liz smiled to show she wasn't offended. 'No need to apologise.'

He gave her the smallest of smiles in return, then turned and started up the street.

She followed him as they moved purposefully in what she thought, but wasn't sure, was the same direction they had the other night. They hadn't gone very far, though, before he took them into the shell of a factory and inside an overseer's office, a tiny brick room standing on its own up against one of the more intact walls. Once he'd made sure there were no gaps in the blackout curtain hanging outside the door, Isaac wound up a lamp, then took dust covers off the desk and the two chairs either side of it and motioned for her to sit down.

She frowned, puzzled, but did as she was bade. 'What are we doing?'

'Waiting.'

'For what?'

'For word.'

'Oh.'

Liz subsided into silence and looked around.

Despite the fact that the factory was an abandoned ruin, the office was relatively clean and tidy. All the furnishings, apart from a very dead potted plant, were covered with thick sheets and corrugated iron had been placed over the office to protect it from the elements. The windows that had once looked out over the factory floor had been boarded up with wooden planks to stop light from escaping, as had the glass pane in the door. Even the floor was relatively free of the dust that seemed to be everywhere else. It looked like the space was actually used quite often, but what for, Liz had no idea, especially when Isaac had a perfectly good laboratory and, presumably, somewhere he lived. She had a feeling she would find out soon enough, though.

The boy was watching her, waiting for her to finish, and when he did he stood and went to a filing cabinet in the corner. He pulled back the sheet, then produced a key from a pocket and unlocked the lower drawer. Instead of files there was a large cardboard box inside and he lifted it out with some difficulty and dropped it on his chair. The box was stamped with a War Ministry code and Liz peered in to see it was filled with cans and vacuum packets.

'Are you hungry?' Isaac asked. 'Thirsty?'

'Army rations?' Liz asked.

Isaac gave her a lopsided grin. 'The army doesn't exactly need them right now, do they?'

'I suppose not.' Pretty much the entirety of the army of the Kingdom of Great Britain was currently at home eating fresh food and definitely not the widely detested "consumption-ready meals", or "CRM" ration packs. She had eaten them while on training camps with her family, learning to survive in the wilderness and such, and she agreed with the general opinion that it was better to leave them well alone until you had no other choice. That having been said, there were a couple of really rather good things in the packs and she leaned forward eagerly to peer into the box.

'I don't suppose you have any spotted dick in there?'

Isaac rooted around briefly before producing two cans, which he placed on the table. Liz turned them so she could read the writing stencilled on the sides.

'Tripe?' she asked, suppressing a shudder at the thought of what most considered one of the worst meals in a can the army had ever produced.

Isaac shrugged as he continued to search the box. He eventually found what he was looking for - a very basic tin opener made from a small piece of scrap metal, a couple of which were included in every ration box.

'It reminds me of my dad; it was one of his favourites and an army friend of his used to grab him a few cans every so often.' He gestured at her tins. 'Hot?'

'Yes, please!'

He pressed the buttons on the tops of the cans and there was a whir as the tiny clockwork heaters did their job. The noise stopped after only a few seconds and then Isaac applied the tin opener to Liz's can. The unwieldy blunt implement slipped in his hands several times and failed to make much of a dent. He eventually gave up and tossed it on the table.

'Sorry. I keep meaning to bring a proper opener instead of relying on these... things. I'll have to use a screwdriver.'

'Try this instead.' Liz said, fishing out the *Sheffield Knife* that had been in one of the pockets of the sneak suit.

Isaac's eyes widened at the sight of the compact multi-tooled implement and he smiled as he took it. He turned the tiny dial on it to select the tin opener, then pressed the button to make it flick out.

In moments the cans were open and steam was rising in the cooling air.

He closed the tool, but, instead of handing it back immediately, he gazed down at it, his happiness at seeing it gone.

'Your father had one, right?' Liz asked softly.

Isaac nodded and held the tool out mutely.

'Keep it,' Liz said. 'I have another.'

He gaped at her, surprised and delighted in equal parts. 'Thank you!' He turned the tool over in his hands, gazing lovingly at it for a moment, but then set it down on the table next to the cans and pulled a couple of tiny spoons from the box, handing one to Liz.

They dug in and for a while the only sound was the soft scrape of metal on metal.

Liz savoured her food. While there was an abundance of desserts at the palace, especially during formal dinners, they tended to be more on the elaborate side. Which was all well and good, but there was something about the simple suet pudding that just appealed to her and it had been all she'd been able to think about as soon as she'd seen what was in the box.

She shared a smile with Isaac, who was spooning his tripe into his mouth stoically and without much apparent relish. His eyes weren't leaving her for one second, as if he was frightened she was going to disappear if he did. She was used to being watched all the time so it didn't put her off, but that was because she was the Princess of Wales and there were always either guests forced to pay attention to her or servants trying to anticipate her every need. She wasn't sure why Isaac was watching her so closely.

'Awright, Tinker.'

Liz squealed and almost dropped her pudding when someone spoke from just behind her and she only just stopped herself from leaping out of her chair when she saw Isaac's grin. She scowled at him, knowing now why he had been watching her.

'You could have warned me!'

'It wouldn't have been half as much fun if I had. Besides, I wanted to see how quickly you would react; if you want to be a pilot like your cousin you're going to have to have good reactions.'

Liz gave him another glare, then turned in her seat to find the owner of the voice. She wasn't too surprised to find a child; the voice had been too high pitched and soft to be that of an adult, but she was surprised to see how young the girl was. At least she thought it was a girl - it was hard to know for sure under so much grime.

Bright blue eyes peered out from a face that was almost black with muck and turned in Liz's direction.

'Watchoo lookin' at, eh?'

'Sorry, I was just surprised is all.'

The girl stared at Liz, peering up at her with eyes that were far too old for her, before turning to Isaac. 'Oo's the toff?'

'A friend, Ivy. Behave.'

The girl sniffed derisively and wiped her nose on her sleeve, leaving a not quite clean, but at least brighter streak on her cheek.

She glanced sideways at Liz, then returned her attention to Isaac. 'Got eyes on Fritz. Ee's holed up in *Wallingtons*. No sign of the other mark yet. Trotter's watchin' out for 'im, ee'll send word.'

Isaac nodded solemnly. 'Thank you.' He held out six of the tins from the box. 'Here.'

The girl gave Liz as wide a berth as she could as she went to take the cans. They disappeared one by one inside her filthy clothing.

'Eat some yourself, this time. Don't give it all to your brother,' Isaac instructed.

The girl wrinkled her nose and shrugged. 'Ee's a growin' lad, ee needs it.'

'You need it too or you'll be too weak to take care of him.' Isaac gave her a stern look, which had no apparent effect on her whatsoever. Eventually, he just sighed. 'Tell the others they can come by the lab to get theirs tomorrow.'

'Awright. Will do, Tink.' The girl said. She looked Liz up and down once more, shook her head in disapproval, then slipped around the blackout curtain on the door, barely disturbing it.

Liz huffed. 'I don't think she likes me.'

Isaac grinned. 'Ivy doesn't like anyone being with me, especially if they're female.'

Liz raised an eyebrow. 'She's jealous? She must be all of ten years old!'

Isaac shrugged. 'Eight. The war makes children grow up quickly. Her brother is four and she's the only thing stopping him from starving. She's proud and insists on paying her way, no matter how much I offer to help them.'

'And you have other children working for you?'

Isaac nodded. 'Including Ivy and her brother, twenty-nine. Mostly orphans, but a couple are looking after an invalid parent or grandparent. None of them want to leave their homes even though most of them are bombed out. And none of them want to be pitied,' he warned as Liz frowned. 'They just want to be useful.'

'And they do what? Spy on spies?' Liz asked with a wry smile.

'They're my eyes and ears. So, yes. Among other things' He leaned down and took a notebook out from under a small pile of ceramic tiles. 'I write down everything they report.' He tapped the notebook. 'Every suspicious event they witness and all the criminal activity: the army trucks that deliver to private warehouses; the boats that dock at three in the morning after the air raids have ended; the strangers that wander into the neighbourhood. For example,' he turned the pages. 'Our man, Bamford, and the Prussian have met quite a few times, that I know of, anyway, always in a different place.' He showed her the page with its neatly annotated days and times. 'Going back about a year, since just after...' his voice caught and he swallowed and took a deep breath before continuing. 'Since just after the bombings began.'

He bent and put the notebook under the tiles again, making sure it was completely hidden.

'Why keep that here and not in your workshop?'

'Because I have Mr Turner's activities in here as well,' he said, barely audibly, as if frightened the man might be listening.

Liz lowered her voice to match. 'If you know he's carrying out illegal activity why do you work for him? And why do you let him treat you so badly?'

'I don't have a choice.' Isaac mumbled, staring into his can. 'My father was a great scientist, but a terrible businessman. He made a few bad choices and lost a lot of money.'

He stabbed his spoon into his food and lifted some out, but then just put it back in and slid the can onto the table without eating. 'When my father died, the bank took just about everything - the manor, the estate in Devonshire, the townhouse here. All that was left was the factory and the laboratory and I was happy with that; I didn't want or need anything else. But then, just a few days later, Mr Turner showed up with papers saying my dad had taken out loans with him using the factory as collateral. I begged him to let me keep the laboratory at least and he offered me a choice - either I signed the factory and the lab over to him as per the conditions of the loans, or I went to work for him to pay off the debt. I didn't care about the factory, and it's been bombed to bits now anyway, but I didn't want to lose the lab and all my dad's work so I agreed.'

Liz nodded. 'I can understand that. Your father was a genius. It would be a crime for his work to be lost or end up in the hands of unscrupulous people. Where is it, though? I didn't see it in your laboratory.'

'I gave it all to the Royal Institution.'

Liz blinked in surprise. 'You didn't want to keep it?'

'No. I never understood much of what my dad did so it would just be gathering dust in the lab. They said they'll preserve it all with the rest of their artefacts and that I could go see it at any time.' He shrugged. 'At least this way someone can get some use out of it and maybe continue his work.'

Liz nodded; the Royal Institution was the perfect place for Peter Richardson's work to be kept. None of it would be lost or stolen and his research would be available to the scientific community as a whole. 'That's...

'Tinker!' a tiny voice came from behind the blackout curtain. 'He's here! Trotter says he's just gone past Bailey's.'

'Thank you, Will.' Isaac called out to the unseen child. 'We'll start moving. Keep me updated, please!'

'Alright!'

Isaac smiled at Liz. 'It seems the word has been given. Shall we?'

8

Liz scoffed down the rest of her pudding while Isaac returned the room to how it had been and a couple of minutes later they were picking their way through rubble-strewn streets in the general direction of the factories where the two men had been spotted. They hadn't gone far before a tiny child of indeterminate gender appeared to report that the Prussian had started moving and Isaac adjusted their course accordingly. They still didn't know exactly where they were going, though, until a boy, who Isaac greeted as Trotter, showed up and told them that the Prussian had stopped and was waiting in an alleyway.

'That's a tight alleyway,' Isaac mused as they hurried through the darkness after the boy had gone on his way, 'we're going to have to go into one of the buildings flanking it, but neither of them are damaged at all, so they'll be locked up.'

'All we need is an open window within thirty feet,' Liz said. 'Is that possible?'

Isaac thought for a moment, then smiled. 'How about twenty feet above them?'

'That'll do!' Liz answered with a grin, but then had to stop talking and concentrated on putting one foot in front of the other as she started to feel the effects of the quick march across broken ground. She was also starting to regret the pudding as she felt the beginnings of a stitch under her ribs.

Thankfully, they didn't have very far left to go and only a few minutes later they slipped into a factory through a side door, opened for them by yet another small child.

'The Prussian is in the alley behind that wall,' Isaac whispered, pointing to the opposite side of the factory.

Liz peered into the darkness, but what little light coming from the moon and searchlights didn't extend any further than a few feet into the building and she couldn't see beyond the first row of machinery.

There were a few clicks and a pool of light slowly spread on the floor around their feet from a wind-up torch in Isaac's hands.

'Sorry, we can't risk any more light than this.'

The light wasn't nearly enough to illuminate their surroundings, but at least they would be able to see where they were putting their feet. It was also enough to make the face of the child who'd let them in shine palely.

'Welcome to 'Alifax's!' the boy squeaked. 'Me ma was the foreman and I know the factory like the back of me 'and. Whaddya need? I know all the best hiding places.'

Isaac smiled at him. 'We'll keep that in mind, thank you, Charlie. But, for now, do you think you can take us up to somewhere above the Prussian with a window or vent?'

The boy nodded. 'Easy! The berk is standing right underneath one of the windows in the meeting room!'

Liz chuckled. 'That's convenient!'

'Yeah!' The boy grinned and waved for them to follow him as he set off diagonally across the factory.

Liz kept close to Isaac and watched the floor for obstacles, but beyond a discarded broom and a few crates there weren't any; Halifax's seemed to be one of the few factories in this part of London still in operation and it was clean, as far as factories went, with a complete absence of rubble. The boy didn't seem to need the light and forged ahead confidently. Apparently, he did know the factory as well as he claimed and Liz wondered how often he'd been here when he should have been in school and, more importantly, what had happened to his mother.

'A bomb hit his house.' Isaac answered her unspoken question, his lips only inches from her ear so that the child wouldn't hear. 'Mother, father, grandmother and older sister all killed. He was the only survivor. They put him in an orphanage but he kept running back here and hiding under the machines. The workers take care of him now and I help them feed him.'

'That's awful.'

Isaac shrugged. 'Yes, but it is an all too familiar story right now.'

Their path across the factory floor twisted and turned in the corridors between huge, silent machines and ended at a narrow metal staircase that climbed the side wall. The boy raced up the stairs past tiny landings and catwalks leading to inspection panels on the machines, but Isaac and Liz took their time, Liz huffing and puffing, weighed down under her glidewings and gear. He was waiting for them at the top, shifting impatiently from foot to foot, and put a finger to his lips before starting off again.

The corridor that went around the outside of the wall was made of metal and only slightly wider than the stairs had been. They passed a couple of small offices and a toilet, but the fourth door led to a large meeting room and the boy put his finger to his lips again before pushing through the door.

A large oval table, surrounded by chairs, stood in the middle of the room. A smaller table was against the wall on one side, a large brass tea urn sitting on it along with a tray holding upside down mugs. The wall opposite the door was lined with high windows of frosted glass and the boy pointed at the rightmost of the three.

'Ee's under that one. But don't open it; it squeaks sumthin' rotten. Use the one in the middle.'

'Thank you, John.'

The boy nodded, then left, instantly disappearing into the darkness.

There was just about enough light coming through the windows to see by so Isaac turned off the torch and put it back wherever it had come from before helping Liz to manoeuvre a chair into position below the window. He climbed up on it and carefully opened the window just enough for Liz to poke the microphone through on its telescopic pole after she'd assembled and tested it.

She plugged in the earphones and handed one to Isaac. At first there was nothing to hear, except for occasional scuffing noises, which she assumed was the Prussian moving his feet around, but after a few minutes footsteps approached, resounding in the tight alleyway. Liz had had the gain turned all the way up in the silence, but just the noise of the Englishman's dress shoes on concrete had the needle on the recorder going right off the scale and she turned it down to half. She had to turn it down even further, though, when the men began to speak and she marvelled at how good Scarlet's equipment was.

'*Guten abend, Herr Bamford.*'

'Yes, yes. Good evening to you, too, Schultz. Do you have what I asked for?'

'Why so hasty? Wouldn't you like to enjoy the evening for a few minutes? I have brought cigars and some schnapps. We could drink to your imminent appointment.'

'How do you know about that? That was only decided this weekend!'

The Prussian, Schultz, laughed gently. 'You do not think you are the only one on our payroll in the government, do you?'

'No, of course not,' Bamford bluffed.

The Prussian chuckled again. 'Do not sulk! You are of course our most highly placed and valued asset. After the war minister himself, of course.'

Liz shared a look with Isaac; with just those few words they probably already had enough to convict the war minister of treason. It would be foolish to stop recording the meeting, though; anything they could learn about the Prussian plans would be immeasurably helpful to the British forces and could save countless lives.

There was a brief silence before Bamford spoke again. 'You said you have cigars? I'm not a big fan of schnapps, but I haven't had a decent cigar in months. Can't get them, you see.'

'Here. Best Italian cigars.'

'My word...'

There was another silence and then the click of a lighter and the sound of the two men pulling on their cigars. The pungent smell of smoke wafted up to the window and Liz wrinkled her nose in distaste.

Bamford sighed contentedly. 'That's good...'

'It is not bad. Next time I will bring American and we can compare them.'

'If you insist!' It was Bamford's turn to laugh, an annoying nasal braying sound.

The silence dragged out as the two men smoked for a while longer and Liz eyed the recorder in concern, but she was surprised to see that, even though the conversation seemed to be dragging on with long pauses, the counter showed that it had only recorded ten minutes and there was plenty of magnetic tape left.

'Now, *Herr Bamford*, we can get down to business, if you'd like.'

'Please; I would like to get home before the air raids begin.'

'There will be no raids tonight, so do not concern yourself with that.'

'Oh, jolly good! That's nice to know.'

'Yes, you can stay in bed all night. Whose will it be tonight? Your own with your wife? Or... Which one of your mistresses do you currently favour?'

'It's Betty at the mo... I say, steady on!'

The Prussian laughed cruelly. 'I'm sorry, my little joke.'

'It wasn't funny!'

'I suppose not, but I have very little else to entertain myself with in your country except what little gossip and slander I pick up.' There was another brief silence before the Prussian's voice came again. 'The agreement has been drawn up as you requested and signed by the Kaiser and crown prince.'

'Good. Hand it over then and I'll be on my way.'

There was a laugh. 'I do not have it, of course! It will come over in the diplomatic pouch tomorrow morning, hidden among the papers dealing with prisoners of war.'

'I will inform the minister.'

'*Sehr gut.* Then...'

'Well, well, well, wot've we got 'ere then?'

It took a moment for Liz to realise that the voice she was hearing wasn't coming from the earphone, but from the room behind her. She turned to look just in time to be blinded when a torch came on.

'You two? Wot're you doin' sneakin' around my territory, eh?'

'For pity's sake, turn the light off, Rodney!' Isaac hissed. 'And lower your voice!'

'The other day we was passin' through your territory, but today you're on mine and you don't tell me wot ta do in *my* territory, Richardson!' The smaller of the two shadows growled as they advanced around the conference table. 'An' dontcha dare lift yer arm!' A huge pistol appeared in the light of the torch, clutched in the meaty hand of the largest shadow. 'First sign of ya using that little shooter of yers and me mate Alfie 'ere will blow yer 'ead orf.'

'Yeah!'

'Please!' Liz whispered, holding up her free hand, pleading for then to quieten down, 'you don't understand...!'

'Yeah?' Rodney turned on Liz. 'Wot don' I understand, little Miss Scientist?'

'She's not a scientist!' Isaac said, 'she's the Princess of Wales!'

'Give over!' Rodney scoffed, then rounded on Alfie as the torch bobbed up and down wildly. 'Keep the bloody light still, willya?' He gave the big man a stern glare before turning back. 'Am I really supposed to believe...?'

He was interrupted again when Alfie tapped him on the arm, nearly knocking him over, and thrust a tattered book filled with newspaper cuttings at him. 'What now?'

'Look, Rodney, look!'

The two men started flipping through the book and Liz used the distraction to turn to Isaac. 'You know who I am? How?'

'I went to a reception at the palace with my father a few years back and you spoke to him for a few minutes. He was so happy for days after because you'd obviously read and understood his work. It made an impact on me and I recognised you as soon as I saw you properly in my workshop.'

'Why didn't you say anything?'

Isaac shrugged. 'It seemed important to you that you were someone else.'

'Sorry to interrupt,' Rodney said, rubbing his hands together anxiously as he stepped forward, 'Alfie 'ere is a bit of a monarchist and keeps a scrapbook, so he recognised yer worship an' convinced me it's you.' He bobbed his head obsequiously. 'So, we're not gonna kill yers like we woz gonna, but we will have to rough yer boy there up a bit. For the principal, like. Y'know?'

Alfie handed the gun to Rodney, who held it on them as the big man advanced. He grabbed Isaac by the collar of his coat and picked him up bodily.

'Wait!' Liz cried, clawing at Alfie in an attempt to stop him, but she might as well have been trying to stop a lorry and the man took no notice and slammed his hand into Isaac's belly.

The breath went out of Isaac and he wriggled and tried to curl into a ball, but Alfie just kept his grip on him, holding him in mid-air as easily as if he were a kitten. He pulled his hand back and prepared another punch, this time to Isaac's face, but before he could strike the lights in the room went on.

Liz shaded her eyes and squinted across the room to where three man-sized shadows had appeared. Her eyes, already abused by the torch, adjusted quickly and she was horrified to see that the man in the middle was the Prussian, Schultz. Worse, all three men had pistols.

She edged her hand towards the recorder, reaching for the buttons which would stop the recording and cut and wrap the tape so that she could hide it.

'Do not move, please, Miss.'

Schultz's pistol swung towards her and she froze.

'Now, this is a very interesting situation.' The Prussian said, looking first at Rodney, whose pistol had turned towards him, then at Liz, before finishing on Alfie and Isaac. He smiled. 'We have two, um, *colourful* locals who seem to be displeased with the behaviour of two children. Children who appear to have been recording my private and very sensitive conversation in the street outside for some reason. Very interesting!'

''Oo the 'ell are you?'

'I am the man who has money in his pocket,' the Prussian answered, slowly reaching into his inside pocket and pulling a thick sheaf of pound notes out. He threw it on the table. 'It is yours if you leave now.'

Rodney stared down at the money for a good few seconds, his eyes widening and his tongue wetting his lips, before looking back up at the Prussian. 'I really do like money,' he said, grinning widely. 'A lot.'

'Yeah, a lot.' Alfie echoed.

'*Gut*, then we have a...'

'And I *am* a crook, so I'd do just about anything to get money,' Rodney went on, cutting off the Prussian. He looked over his shoulder at Liz. 'However,' he said. 'We're *British* crooks, we are. We're not flippin' *traitors*.'

The gunshots were deafening in the confined space.

Rodney fired first, but the Prussian had already started moving and he missed. He tried to adjust his aim, but the man on the right turned his gun on him in that moment and he had to dive to the side.

Alfie was the only one of the men without a weapon, but that didn't stop him. As soon as Rodney had fired, he had dropped Isaac and charged at the man on the left. The Prussian's henchman pulled his trigger, but the big man kept going, showing no sign whether the bullet had hit him or not. He crashed into the man and crushed him against the wall. The man had the wind knocked out of him, but tried to bring his gun to bear again. Alfie ignored the weapon and just grabbed him by the head and bashed it repeatedly into the whitewashed bricks. When he finally let go of him the man crumpled lifelessly to the floor, leaving behind a red smear.

When the shots first started going off Liz froze, images of the night her family were attacked by Prussian stormtroopers flashing through her mind. The sight of Isaac curled up and retching on the floor broke the spell, though, and she dropped down next to him.

'Isaac!' She ducked and turned, covering his body and hers with the glidewings, as shots thudded into the table right above them and hit the wall where she'd been standing only moments before.

'I'm alright!' The boy managed to gasp out in a brief silence. 'We have to get out of here!'

'Can you run?'

Isaac uncurled slowly. 'I think so.' He reached out and pulled the recorder towards himself. He unplugged the lead to the microphone and Liz went to collapse the telescopic pole, but it was bent and she couldn't, so she discarded it and just took the microphone.

She looked at Isaac. 'Ready?' she whispered.

Isaac twisted to his knees. 'Ready.'

There were several more shots and a scream, then the room went silent again.

Liz nodded and prepared to spring up, but Isaac looked up at something over her head and deflated.

'Oh, please. Don't go anywhere on my account.'

She spun around and found the Prussian leaning against the far end of the long table. He was slightly hunched over, blood leaking from between the fingers of his right hand as it pressed against his left side under his armpit, but the gun in his left hand was unwavering.

'Put the recorder on the table and slide it down here to me.'

Isaac picked up the recorder and stood.

'Slowly!'

Isaac slid it towards the Prussian and he waved for him to back off with the gun. Isaac did so, raising his arms in surrender.

'Thank you.' The Prussian smiled, then turned the gun on the recorder and fired three shots in rapid succession. It shattered and Liz turned away and shielded her eyes as pieces of machinery and electronics flew in all directions. The Prussian took no notice of her, though, and just poked around in the ruins with the muzzle of his gun. He quickly found what he was looking for and, without taking his eyes from Isaac and Liz, put his gun in his pocket and fished inside. He pulled out the tape and started yanking it free, but it was caught on the mechanisms and resisted.

This time, when his eyes went to the recorder, Isaac was ready. He brought his arms down and extended his right towards the Prussian. There was a soft hiss of compressed air being explosively released and the man cried out and fell back, clutching his face.

'Run!' Isaac shouted, pulling Liz to her feet before bolting for the door.

'The tape!' Liz called.

'Leave it! It's not worth it!'

Liz bit her lip and eyed the recorder at the far end of the table. The tape *was* worth it. It was worth her life, Isaac's life and the life of the two men lying on the floor next to the two Prussians they'd killed.

She went for it.

Three quick steps took her to the recorder, but it took precious seconds for her to gather up all the pieces that were connected by the tangled tape. She clutched them awkwardly to her chest as she edged around the end of the table past the moaning Prussian and shot a triumphant smile at Isaac, who had already made it to the door and was holding it for her. She began to run to him, but before she had gone even a single step a hand grabbed her ankle and she crashed heavily to the floor, the sharp edges of the broken recorder digging painfully into her ribs as the weight of the glidewings bore her down. The hand released her and she tried to get back to her feet, but then whole weight of the Prussian came down on her back and she collapsed again.

'Liz!'

Liz was able to turn her head just enough to see Isaac moving hesitantly towards them, his arm raised as he tried to find a clear shot.

Some of the weight came off her and she caught a glimpse out of the corner of her eye of Schultz lifting his gun towards Isaac. The boy was too close, there was no way the Prussian could miss, unless...

Liz twisted her body with all her strength, flailing wildly with her arm at the same time. She managed to knock the gun, just as it went off, and the bullet struck the wall, missing Isaac by inches. He recoiled back, then gave her an apologetic look before racing out into the darkness of the factory.

'*Verdammt!*' The Prussian cried out. He looked down at her, growled, then lifted the gun over her head.

That was the last thing she saw before the blackout curtains were drawn over her eyes.

9

Liz regained consciousness, but only very briefly, when she was dragged from the meeting room by more Prussians, then again when they rolled her into the boot of an autocar, but it wasn't until she was thrown onto a hard floor that she came fully awake. Despite the shooting pain in her head, made rather worse by having it bounced off the floor, she willed herself to remain limp, pretending to still be unconscious, until the door closed behind her captors. She waited until their voices had faded away completely and only then did she open her eyes and lift her head to look around in the dim light coming from a small light hanging from the beams several metres above her.

She was in a moderately large room with brick walls and a deeply scored wooden floor. A metal door in the middle of one wall seemed to be the only entry or exit. Large windows took up most of one wall, but they were covered with newspapers, blocking her view out. It looked like a storeroom in a factory or warehouse, but it was empty and, judging by the dust her breath was blowing up, hadn't been used for a while.

As for herself, aside from the splitting headache and an ache in her ankle where she might have sprained it when the Prussian had pulled her down, she didn't feel too bad, surprisingly. There was a familiar weight on her back ,which told her she still had her glidewings, but a quick pat down of her pockets revealed that her tools, survival knife and radio were gone. They had even taken her lock picks, but that didn't really matter because she wasn't very far along with her lessons with Scarlet and probably wouldn't have been able to do anything with them anyway.

Her preliminary assessment finished, she rolled onto her side and struggled to her feet, then hobbled to the windows. She pulled aside one of the newspapers to create the smallest of openings and peered out. It was still night - a quick check of her chronograph told her it wasn't quite midnight - and the river running past was a black ribbon flecked with silver. Directly below the window was a large dock, extending out into the water, where cargo ships could unload, so it was a safe bet she was in a warehouse, not a factory. The wrought iron majesty of the Brunel Bridge was to her right and she could just about make out the distinctive shape of Tower Bridge beyond it, meaning she was in Wapping, probably not far from the tube station if she could somehow get to it.

She pressed her forehead to the window in an attempt to see what was directly below. As far as she could tell, there was a forty or fifty foot drop, most likely onto concrete or brick, and no fire escape or other way to climb down.

She abandoned the window and padded silently around the room, the soft-soled boots that had come with the sneak suit making very little noise. There was a large pile of sacks in a corner and she went to inspect them, hoping for something to defend herself with, a cargo hook maybe, like the dock workers used for moving sacks. No such luck, though; it was just a pile of moulding potato sacks, and she backed away from them rapidly when there was a high-pitched squeak and one of them moved.

Her circuit of the room unsatisfactorily concluded, she went to the door and pressed her ear against it. At first she couldn't hear anything beyond the pounding of her heart, but she held still, calming herself, and was eventually rewarded by a laugh. There would be no escape that way.

Her attention went back to the window; even if she couldn't climb out she might be able to attract someone's attention by breaking the glass or shouting. She ripped all the newspaper off and threw it to the floor, then looked out again. There was nobody out there, though. The river was deserted and this late, with no air raid in the offing, anyone who could be at home in bed with their families would be, snatching some rest while they could.

She rested her forehead against the window and sighed, her breath briefly misting the glass. It was her fault she was in this situation; she was the one who had insisted on doing this on her own without bringing along Scarlet or another professional and it was her who had left the Brunel Tower under false pretences, without telling anyone in the palace where she was going or the true reason for going there.

Nobody was coming to save her because nobody knew where she was or even that she was in trouble. So, she was just going to have to save herself.

The middle of the windows had a latch and she wiggled it experimentally, hoping that it wouldn't be locked. It moved slightly and she smiled in relief then pulled at it carefully, not wanting it to squeak and give away the fact that she was awake. It took a bit of effort, but eventually it released and she put her hands on the window frame and pushed gently. The window opened by fits and starts, but eventually it had swung back, leaving almost as large a hole as the windows did in her lab.

Liz held on to the window frame and leaned out as much as she dared to inspect the wall below her. Unfortunately, it was just a plain brick wall, featureless until it ended at the large wooden doors of a loading bay twenty or so feet below. There was no way she could climb down, but climbing up wasn't an option either. There was a beam sticking out from the wall above the window that looked like it might once have held a pulley for swaying up sacks like the ones in the pile in the corner, but there was no pulley and no ropes and the beam was too far away for her to use as a stepping stone to get to the roof.

She was stuck.

She sat down where she was and put her back to the wall under the window. It wasn't exactly comfortable with the glidewings, so she started to unbuckle them, but then stopped.

She looked up over her shoulder at the window, then rolled her eyes at herself for being stupid.

She checked the power gauge on the motor of the glidewings - it had about half charge, which was easily enough for what she had in mind.

She stood and looked at the window again, measuring it with her eyes. The gap was wide, but not wide enough for her to go through with the glidewings fully extended, which meant the fans would be covered. Once through, she'd have to extend the wings as quickly as she could so they could produce lift. Only having forty feet to play with would make it a very delicate operation indeed and the margin for error would be minimal if she wanted to hold onto enough altitude to make good her escape. However, even if she failed, the worst that should happen was a hard landing; the glidewings, even partially extended, should prevent the fall from being fatal. If it came to that then she might at least be able to lose herself in the surrounding streets and alleyways.

With nothing to lose and everything to gain there was no question as to what she was going to do, so she pulled tight the straps of the glidewings, then backed away to the far side of the room. She pulled the lever to extend the first two panels of the glidewings and set her feet like a runner waiting for the off, then turned the motor on and rotated the knob slowly, adding power to the fans. At first everything seemed fine, but, as they sped up, a worrying vibration began. For a moment she thought that the fans had been damaged again, but it didn't feel like it had when they'd broken before - the vibration was too regular, too deep and there was an almost pleasant resonance to it that wasn't really consistent with damaged parts. The vibration was increasing as the fans whirred faster and faster, threatening to shake her teeth out of her gums and she realised that it was coming from the fans themselves - the thrust they were creating had nowhere to go and was rebounding on them, shaking the blades in their casings. She almost stopped there, frightened of what would happen to her if the fans shook themselves apart whilst going so fast, but they *had* to be powered up before she jumped, otherwise she'd have no chance of staying in the air, so she kept pouring on the power, praying they would stay intact just a little while longer. The vibration didn't get any worse, but the fans began to emit a screeching noise that made her fear for their continued existence.

That was her signal to stop pushing her luck.

She left the knob where it was, took a deep breath to prepare herself, then started pounding heavily across the room towards the windows.

However, before she'd taken more than a couple of steps, the door burst open and two men appeared. They shouted and sprinted towards her.

Liz redoubled her efforts, lowering her head and leaning forward to reduce the drag of the wings.

The window was only a yard away and she gathered herself to leap, but, just as she was about to do so, something heavy hit her from the side and she fell and slid along the floor. Something gave in the glidewings as she crashed into the wall underneath the windows and the right wing bent almost perpendicular.

Before she had time to recover her wits, Liz found a pistol shoved in her face.

'Turn it off.' The man shouted over the increasingly strident sound of the stricken fans.

Without taking her eyes off the gun, Liz groped underneath her for the button controlling the motor. She pressed it and after one last agonised screech there was silence. The two Prussians grabbed her under the arms and pulled her to her feet. They cut through the straps of the glidewings then stripped them from her and threw them in the corner with a clang. Rope was produced and they hogtied her, painfully binding her arms and feet together behind her.

They were about to leave her there when one of them laughed and pointed to the sacks in the corner. He went and grabbed one, then fed it over Liz's head, blinding her and almost choking her with the smell of must and mould.

They laughed again, then she heard the sound of their feet crossing the wooden floor and the door thumped shut behind them.

The first instinct of most people in her situation would be to panic and struggle against their bonds, which would only serve to make them tighter and harder to deal with. At least, that was what she'd been told by an army instructor who'd been brought in before she'd gone to work at the depot to teach her a few classes about what to do in the event that someone tried or succeeded in kidnapping her. However, knowing that struggling was the worst thing she could do and stopping herself from doing so were two very different things, especially with the sack over her head restricting her breathing and with what little air she could gasp in rank with mould and what was probably rat doings. It would have been all too easy to lose what little control over herself she had left after her escape attempt had been foiled, but she wouldn't allow herself to do so; too much depended on her getting free and, besides, not all was lost. She was still holding a few cards up her sleeve, or rather, in her shoes.

The position the Prussians had left her in was desperately uncomfortable and extremely restricting, but it did put her hands very close to her boots and it was only a matter of finding some leverage for her to reach the blade secreted in the heel of the right one. She managed to get her fingers to it and started working it free.

'If you get into a knife fight expect to get cut.' Scarlet had told her when she'd shown Liz the little surprises hidden about the sneak suit, all the while making one of the blades from her own boots dance over her knuckles. She had made the knife disappear, then reappear a few times before launching it backhanded across the lab to stick into the evacuation map on the back of the door, fully thirty feet away. 'And if you're going to use a knife to cut yourself free, then a bit of pain and blood is a small price to pay for your life.'

The knife wasn't meant to be a weapon, unless the agent was truly desperate, instead it was meant for precisely the use Liz intended for it. The blade was wafer thin and it had an extremely small handle, which was basically just a small piece of leather, making it almost undetectable to a normal search, but also extremely hard to grasp and wield. It was also incredibly sharp and Liz pursed her lips in concentration, willing to suffer a few cuts, but not lose the tips of her fingers. After several minutes of patient manipulation it came free of its sheath and she palmed it, hissing as she earned her first cut at the base of her thumb. Ignoring the stinging pain and the liquid that welled up around the cut, she slowly turned the knife until the blade was pointing the other way, then pushed it into the ropes. She felt a few strands part and grinned in triumph, but then the knife slipped in her fingers and almost fell. She managed to catch it before it tumbled away, but got another cut for her hubris.

She manoeuvred the knife back into position, then started to poke and prod. Sawing was impossible with no leverage, but the point of the blade was so sharp that she could essentially dig through the rope. Blood was now making the knife slippery, but the leather tab on the end was just enough for her to get a grip on and she persevered.

Strand after strand parted and eventually, after how long she had no idea, one of the ropes parted and she felt the bonds around her legs loosen.

She swore softly; she'd been working at the wrong ropes. Freeing her feet wasn't going to help her very much.

She held the knife carefully in her left hand and used the right to pull apart the ropes around her legs, freeing them, then stretched herself out, relieving the pressure on her back. She enjoyed the sensation of increased freedom for only a moment, though, before going back to work.

With slightly more mobility the process was much quicker and the ropes fell away in no time. She dropped the knife and stripped the ropes away as she sat up, then scrabbled at the sack. She ripped it off and gulped down the clean, cool night air coming through the window.

'Bravo!'

Liz spun around and found Schultz sitting on the floor against the wall next to the door. He had a bandage around his head and another was visible under his open shirt and jacket, wrapped around his ribs. Both were red where blood had seeped through.

He gave her a smile. 'You have an interesting skill set and strange accoutrements. Not quite what I would expect from a princess - tapes in lieu of tiaras, glidewings instead of gowns...'

'Princess? I'm not a...'

Liz trailed off when the Prussian waved Alfie's scrapbook at her. One corner of it was stained red. He opened it up and showed her a picture of herself. It looked like one from a gala she'd attended a few months before, at the Royal Albert Hall.

'I do not understand the obsession that common English people have with royalty.' The man shook his head, perplexed, then snapped the book shut and tossed it into the corner of the room where it landed on top of the sacks.

'Forgive me for not greeting or treating you as protocol demands.'

'I think we're beyond such niceties,' Liz said, wincing at the pain shooting through her head as she pushed herself up to a sitting position, 'and I wouldn't expect such behaviour from a Prussian, anyway, after you invaded my home. I assume you ran that operation?'

The man tilted his head. 'I had a part in it, yes, but I did speak against it.'

'I don't believe you.'

'Not all Prussians are fanatics, or narcissistic killers only looking out for their own interests, like Hans Gruber. Most of us are merely patriots, fighting for our country. For our Kaiser. He says this war is necessary, so whether we believe in it or not is irrelevant, it is just what we are honour-bound to do. Much like your British soldiers, I would presume.'

'Inciting treason amongst our politicians isn't exactly honourable.'

Schultz shrugged. 'If your politicians were honourable I wouldn't be able to incite treason amongst them.' He reached behind himself and pulled an ashtray from the darkness beyond the doorway. It was a large metal ashtray, such as they had in pubs, and the magnetic tape from her recorder was piled on it. A lighter was with it and he clicked it to life. 'And, I'm sorry, but I will have to continue to do so.'

He touched the lighter to the tape, recoiling slightly as it flared, combusting spectacularly. In moments it was ash and he waved away the smoke with a cough, then pushed the ashtray to the side.

'I would do anything to help the Prussian Empire win the war quickly. That way the killing will stop as soon as possible.'

'An admirable sentiment,' Liz said, keeping her tone neutral, but pouring all her scorn and vitriol into her words as only an Englishwoman, and one of undeniable class, could, 'but completely invalid as justification for your acts and those of your countrymen. The Prussian Empire, as the aggressors in this war, could end things tomorrow by just going home.'

Schultz's eyes widened in surprise and he was silent for a moment, but then he laughed. 'Well, it was worth a try, but I suppose I may as well give up on the "nice guy" routine.' Any pretence at amiability disappeared and his eyes turned cold. 'I have so very many questions and I do hope you'll answer them without me having to ask my men to come in and ask you more insistently.' He gave her a cruel smile. 'So... How did you find out about tonight's meeting? Who betrayed me?'

Liz gave him one of the condescending smiles she reserved for particularly obnoxious politicians. 'Well, actually, it was the war minister. He regrets what he has done to this country and wants to make amends.'

The Prussian laughed again, a mirthless barking sound that set Liz's already abused teeth on edge. 'Very amusing! But I do not think so.' He gave her a calculating look. 'I do not believe we were betrayed, which means it must have been an accident. But you, you do not belong here. It would not be you who would discover me.' He paused, tapping his lips with a finger thoughtfully. 'I have felt eyes on me before and thought it was my imagination, but now I think not.' He pointed the finger at her. 'That boy. It was him, wasn't it?'

Liz tried to remain composed and not give anything away, but she must have done because Schultz's eyes lit up in triumph.

'Aha! Yes! Who is he?'

'Just a soldier. My bodyguard.'

'No, no, no. He wasn't dressed like a soldier. Didn't move like a soldier...' He tapped his lips with his finger again. 'He is one of the children I have seen sneaking around late at night, yes?' He smiled coldly. 'He has local knowledge and would have led you to me. Which means he most likely lives around here. It will not be hard to find him, I think.'

He grinned again. 'I am enjoying this! It has been too long since I have been able to test my intellect with such a puzzle.'

'Perhaps we can play chess next?'

'Ha! Very good! But I think not.' He chuckled, shaking his head, but then his expression changed once more and his voice became harsher than ever. 'Last question. And I urge you to answer this one properly.'

The man leaned forward to peer closer at Liz. 'You were recording, so you obviously still need proof of the war minister's treachery,' he tapped the metal ashtray on the floor next to him with a ragged fingernail, 'but you didn't get it tonight. So, who will come to get that proof if you do not return? Who else did you tell that you were coming here?'

Liz looked down at the scarred wooden floorboards beneath her, hiding her face as she racked her mind for an answer that would satisfy him enough that he wouldn't kill or torture her. The trouble was, she had a feeling that one or both of those things were in her future, no matter what she said.

'Last chance, Princess.' Schultz snarled impatiently. 'Who did you tell?'

'Me.'

In an evening packed with shocks and surprises, it seemed there was still room for one more and Liz gasped as Scarlet jumped down from the window and landed next to her with a soft thud. She wasn't as surprised as Schultz, though, and the man jerked back, banging his head on the wall. He fumbled in his coat for a weapon, but Scarlet tutted and shook her head as a gun appeared in her hand.

'While I would like an excuse to shoot you, I think my boss would rather question you while you were still alive.'

Schultz sighed, then slowly pulled his hand out of his coat and raised both of them.

'Thank you.' Scarlet gave him a wide grin.

'He has more men in the factory.' Liz said urgently, struggling to her feet.

'Already taken care of.' Scarlet said without looking away from the Prussian. 'You alright?'

'I'm a bit banged up, but nothing serious.' Liz said, but then frowned. 'Did you put some kind of tracking device in my suit?'

Scarlet laughed. 'Course not! Even *our* budget doesn't go that far! But we didn't need to; we had the best trackers in London out looking for you.' She lifted her chin towards the doorway behind the Prussian.

Liz followed her gaze just as several soldiers streamed into the room, their weapons raised, ready for trouble, torches illuminating every corner of the room in their search for enemies. They weren't who the Misfit Squadron pilot was talking about, though, because there was a familiar figure standing just outside, peering in, his hands in the pockets of his long coat.

'Isaac!'

The boy smiled and came forward at a wave from Scarlet. His eyes were fixed on Liz, so he didn't see the ashtray on the floor until he tripped over it. He looked down at it, puzzled.

Liz went to join him and peered down at the tape, hoping that some of it would be salvageable, but it was ash.

'He burnt the tape in front of me,' she said. 'We don't have the proof we needed.'

'Oh, I wouldn't say that.' Isaac said with a grin. He brought his hand out of his pocket and opened it up to reveal a tiny cylinder, wrapped in wax paper. 'I told you it wasn't worth it to try to get the recorder.'

Liz took it from him. 'How...? When did you...?'

Isaac smiled, but harsh laughter cut him off before he could say answer any of Liz's questions.

Schultz was laughing as two soldiers picked him up off the floor and placed him on his feet. He laughed as they dragged him from the room and he was still laughing as he was frogmarched down the stairs to the factory floor.

'Interesting character,' Scarlet said, coming over to them after ordering the soldiers to start clearing up.

'I thought you were on a mission.' Liz said.

Scarlet gave her a lopsided grin. 'And *I* thought it might be best to hang around London tonight, so I sent someone else and went to have a cup of tea in the barricade where you showed up a few nights ago. I'd already called for backup when we heard the gunfire and one of Isaac's young friends found me there with a couple of squads of soldiers, just about to send out search parties.'

A soldier came in and stood to attention a few feet from them. He waited for Scarlet to look at him, then saluted. 'Building is clear, ma'am, and the prisoners are ready for transport.'

Scarlet returned the salute. 'Thank you, sergeant.'

The soldier nodded, then saluted Liz. 'Ma'am.'

He turned to go, but Liz called out to stop him. 'Sergeant Wilson! Good to see you again.'

The man snapped back to attention and smiled broadly, extremely pleased that she'd recognised him. 'You too, ma'am!'

'Thank you for coming to my rescue again.'

'You're very welcome, ma'am!'

Liz nodded and the man saluted again, then marched smartly out.

'We should be going,' Scarlet said, 'the palace is worried and we have a lot to do. First, though,' she held out her hand.

'Of course.' Liz said, handing her the tape.

Scarlet held it up between thumb and forefinger and gazed at it. 'A few years ago I was a farmer in County Galway. I never dreamed I'd hold the fate of the nation in my hand.' She threw the tape up into the air, then caught it and made it vanish.

'Right!' she said, grinning and rubbing her hands together eagerly. 'I think we all know what has to be done, but I've got a good idea how to do it and have some fun at the same time!'

The Irishwoman wrapped her arms around Liz and Isaac and walked them out.

10

Regis Reginald Rufus Cummerbund, the Minister of War for the Kingdom of Great Britain strode through the hallways of the Palace of Westminster. There was a spring in his step, or at least as much a spring in his step as there could be for a man who had just turned seventy and had the weight of a country at war bearing down on him.

Today was the day. Finally he would have the reassurances he needed to make a move towards peace on reasonable terms.

He exchanged a few words with the few ministers whose paths he crossed, all early risers like him, but didn't pause or allow them to drag him into any discussions, pleading the need to work on a speech for the upcoming session. He didn't stop until he had gotten to his chambers and closed the door of his office behind him, having told his secretary not to disturb him for at least fifteen minutes.

The satchel was on his desk, as it was every Tuesday, having been flown across the channel by the special red and white striped diplomatic aircraft that was run by the neutral Swiss government for an extortionate fee. He didn't go straight to it, though. Instead, he went to the drinks table against the wall and poured himself a small measure of his favourite Scotch. He began to put the stopper back in the bottle, then reconsidered and poured himself a more generous measure. He took the glass to the window and sipped at the amber liquid while looking out at the Thames flowing by, sparkling in the early morning sunlight.

There was only so long he could savour the moment, though, and after only a minute or so his impatience won out and he downed the rest of his drink and hurried to his desk.

He smiled as he pulled the satchel to himself, but then froze when he saw that the wax seal had been broken. He turned it so that the flap was towards him, flipped it open and tore the contents from it, scattering them over the desk. He found the brown paper packet containing the prisoner of war reports and ripped it open, strewing them haphazardly over the desk. He pushed the papers around, not caring if he bent them or sent them fluttering to the ground, but the agreement wasn't there.

'Have you misplaced something, Minister?'

Cummerbund lifted his head slowly, then turned.

Sitting in one of the armchairs in front of the fireplace on the other side of the room, was the king. His arms were resting on the armrests and he had a sheet of paper in his lap.

'Your Majesty! I didn't see you there.' Cummerbund frowned; there was no fire, because it was summer, so the chairs were in shadow, but still, he should have noticed the king as soon as he'd come in. Then again he had been rather preoccupied. 'Uh, no, no. Just, uh, sorting through the diplomatic pouch.'

'Ah, is that so?' the king picked up the piece of paper. 'Then you weren't looking for this?'

Cummerbund stared at the paper, his eyes going to the red seal with the black eagle at the bottom of the page.

So near but yet so far.

'No. What is that?'

'This,' the king said, laying the paper back onto his knee with care, 'is proof of your treason.'

'Treason?' Cummerbund scoffed. 'I've never seen that before in my life!'

'Of course you haven't! It only arrived today. Direct from Berlin. But it was drawn up to meet your requirements.'

Cummerbund shook his head. 'I don't know where you're getting your information, Your Majesty, but I assure you that it is erroneous. And anyway, even if it were to be the case, a piece of paper is not proof enough of treason on its own.'

'On its own, no. But we have a recording of the meeting between your assistant and a Herr Schultz of Prussian intelligence to back it up, as well as Mr Bamford's signed confession. *That* is enough, if not to see you hang, then to at least remove you from office, effective immediately.'

Cummerbund felt the blood draining from his face and he clutched at the side of his desk as his knees went weak. He pulled himself together quickly, though, and walked across the room to the side table. He lifted the bottle of whisky to the king, offering, but the king shook his head.

'A little too early for me, thank you.'

Cummerbund shrugged and poured himself another generous measure then went to the other armchair. Not trusting his legs to lower him into the chair with dignity, he perched on the side of an arm.

'All I wanted to do was save British lives.'

'By betraying the Misfits?'

'All they do is give false hope and prolong the inevitable, so yes, I betrayed them.' Cummerbund pointed a shaking finger at the paper. 'They were a small price to pay to earn the concessions in that document. To save countless British lives.'

'Well, your desire to save lives is an admirable sentiment and one that I think most of us share,' the king said, unknowingly echoing his daughter's response to much the same statement, 'but that was never the way to go about it.' He gestured at the paper. 'And neither is this.'

The king stood and went to the door. He opened it to reveal two military guard officers. 'Thank you, captain, you may carry on.'

The officers saluted, then stomped across the room. The leader of the two, a captain, stopped in front of Cummerbund and glared down at him. 'Regis Reginald Rufus Cummerbund, you are under arrest. Please come with me.'

Cummerbund drained his glass, then tossed it into the fireplace with a casual flick of his wrist, before standing. He said nothing more, though, and just held his head high as he walked from the room.

The king watched them until they left the outer office, then closed the door. He went to the side table and searched the bottles. Finding what he was looking for, he poured a couple of fingers, but didn't pick up the glass. He returned to the armchair and placed the paper in his lap again.

'Squadron Leader Flynn?' he called out to the room, 'I know you're there. I have a job for you.'

The king had known that Scarlet would be able to resist being in at the kill, but he frowned when not one but two shadows detached themselves from the wall beside the large bookcases behind the war minister's desk. His frown deepened further when he saw that the second shadow belonged to his eldest daughter.

'I do hope you have not been teaching my daughter more things that a future queen shouldn't know.'

'Of course not!' Scarlet said as she padded across the room. She picked up the glass and saluted the king with it. 'I'm teaching her things that any self-respecting girl should know.'

The king groaned, but his smile didn't disappear.

Scarlet knocked back the drink - a fifty year-old Irish whiskey that cost as much per bottle as a Spitsteam did to build - then smacked her lips. 'That's not bad. Not bad at all.' She put the glass down and eyed the bottle longingly, but then looked up at the king. 'Sorry, you wanted me to do something?'

'I need you to find to Dame Lennox.' The king replied. 'Tell her that I need to see her, please.'

'Yes, sir!' Scarlet grinned and gave him a salute that was more a cheeky wave than anything remotely martial, then skipped out of the room.

The door closed behind her, leaving Liz and her father alone. He looked at her and sighed. 'Now then, Elizabeth. What am I supposed to do with you?'

'Do with me, father?'

'Well, this kind of behaviour isn't exactly becoming of a princess or the heir to the throne... Is there anything I can say that would persuade you not to leave the palace ever again? At least until the war is over?'

Liz grinned. 'I'm afraid not.'

'Oh, well.' The king sighed, then returned her grin. 'I am so very proud of you.'

'Thank you, father. Now about my reward...'

The king raised his eyebrows. 'Reward?'

'Yes. I think I deserve a reward for saving the kingdom.'

'Did you have something in mind?'

'Isaac should have a laboratory in the Brunel Tower. There's one free on the sixth floor, or he could share mine...'

'I'd like to meet this boy,' the king looked around, peering into the corners of the room, 'he's not here too, is he?'

'No, he was too shy, but I'll bring him to the palace soon.'

'Please do!'

'In the meantime...?'

'Yes, yes, he can have the laboratory on the sixth floor. And we will act on the information in his ledger.'

'Thank you, father.'

'Anything else?'

'The children. If Isaac comes here they will be left without protection.'

'Hmm.' The king stroked his beard again, seriously this time. 'Yes, something really must be done about them and others like them. No child should fall through the cracks like they have. No person should. Perhaps you and I can work with Isaac on a solution that would satisfy everyone.'

'I think that is a wonderful idea, father.'

Liz smiled.

Small steps.

More every day.

THE RISE AND FALL
OF
REGIS REGINALD
RUFUS CUMMERBUND

AUGUST 1941

THE RISE AND FALL OF REGIS REGINALD RUFUS CUMMERBUND

From The Times special evening edition, 19th August 1941

War Minister's Treason Exposed
His Majesty Addresses Parliament

The Palace of Westminster has not been witness to such remarkable scenes as were represented this morning since that fateful day of the fifth of November in the year 1605, as the Minister of War for the Kingdom of Great Britain, The Right Honourable Regis Cummerbund, leader of His Majesty's Government, was arrested in his office by military guard officers in the presence of the king himself. No explanation for the arrest was given at the time to those members of parliament who were on hand and the war minister himself declined to make any comment as he was removed from the premises and taken to an undisclosed location, however, an announcement was made shortly after that the king would address parliament later that morning.

The House of Commons was, understandably, therefore, packed to capacity at ten when the king entered, with every member in good health present and the gallery filled with spectators and representatives of the press. It was the first time that His Majesty had entered the house since the war minister had removed him from his dual positions as the head of government and leader of the war effort and he didn't go to his seat at the far end of the chamber, instead he stood between the members at the table and laid various items upon it.

There is not sufficient room to reproduce His Majesty's address verbatim here, but readers may find it elsewhere in this periodical. However, for the sake of this article, the most pertinent points that were brought up are as follows:

That the war minister has been collaborating with the Prussians for some time, feeding them information on the movements of the British armed forces and Misfit Squadron in particular.

That the war minister has brokered a deal with Kaiser Wilhelm II whereby, in return for the surrender of the Kingdom of Great Britain, Cummerbund will become a puppet ruler and be awarded with lands in both Britain and Prussia.

That as a result of these actions coming to light, the war minister has been charged with high treason and removed from office.

Some of the war minister's staunchest supporters were heard to protest several times during the speech. However, they were rendered silent when His Majesty presented his evidence, in the form of the items he had brought with him.

First was a document bearing the seals and signatures of both Wilhelm II and the crown prince, setting down the terms of the surrender of the Kingdom of Great Britain and the war minister's subsequent reward, exactly how the king had already stated. The speaker of the house was invited to read it aloud and several members of the house were brought forward to authenticate the seals and signatures so that there could be no doubt.

The second piece of evidence was a tape recording of a covert meeting between a Prussian spy, now in custody and identified as Oberst (Captain) Schultz of Prussian intelligence, and one of the war minister's aides, Oswald Bamford. It was played in its entirety and a transcript was provided to the members of the press and is reproduced within this special edition.

The third piece of evidence was a signed confession by Bamford, laying down his role as the war minister's liaison with the Prussian intelligence officer and stating that the contents of the recording had not been fabricated in any way. He went on to name the war minister's co-conspirators, most of whom, this periodical has since learnt, have already been arrested, although a manhunt is under way for those that were able to flee. Bamford also stated in his confession that the war minister had been forced to bring up the schedule by which the surrender would be finalised by the imminent entry of Japan into the war, as announced only an hour earlier by Her Royal Highness, The Princess of Wales in a special broadcast on the KBC.

His Majesty finished his address to the house by stating that it was necessary for their esteemed members to find a replacement for the war minister as soon as possible and that he would give their chosen representative his every support.

Before the applause for the king had even begun to die down, the proposal that he resume his position was already on the table and had been loudly seconded by most of the members. The speaker declared that under such pressing circumstances a popular vote would be acceptable and the king was indeed returned to the position that we now know was unjustly taken from him.

The king graciously accepted the appointment and took his seat. His first act was to reinstate Misfit Squadron and to order their immediate rearming. His second was to disband the war minister's cabinet, some of whom were conspicuously absent, and he stated that he would begin to reconstitute his own that very afternoon. He then declared the sitting over, but invited the leaders of the house to meet with him in his chambers immediately afterwards.

His Majesty was given a standing ovation as he left and the mood in the house, before it dispersed for lunch, was far more optimistic than this correspondent has witnessed in weeks.

A FLYING VISIT

AUGUST 1941

A FLYING VISIT

Lady Penelope Bagshot skipped down the marble stairs, pulling on her thin leather flying gloves as she went. She stopped in the middle of the atrium, in the bright summer sunlight streaming through the large doors.

'I'm just popping out for a while, Biffy!' she called out to her husband.

'Don't be long!' his voice came back to her from the direction of the drawing room. 'Don't forget: we have the locals coming for dinner!'

'I won't!'

She turned and strode through the doors and onto the patio. Her chief fitter, Alasdair Patterson, was waiting just outside, her helmet, with the lenses already attached, cradled carefully in his hands. She took it and strapped it on as she walked down the steps to the lawn.

'Thank you, Alasdair. Is Kingfisher ready?'

'Yes, ma'am. We didn't have time to rewind her completely after this morning, but she'll get you to London nae problem. But I'm worried about how you're going to...'

'Oh, don't fuss,' Penelope said, cutting him off, 'I know what I'm doing.'

Patterson grimaced. 'Yes, ma'am.'

The aircraft was right at the bottom of the steps, where the grass of the immaculate-until-about-a-minute-ago lawn began and she strode around it, giving it an extremely quick check. She winced when she saw a few fresh scratches, but they were nothing to be concerned about as far as her airworthiness was concerned. She'd asked Alasdair to bring

Kingfisher up to the mansion while she'd changed back into her flightsuit to save her a few minutes, but hadn't thought about what the road would do to the aircraft. Since she'd been posted to Scotland the gravel road between the mansion and the airfield hadn't been used much, if at all, and nobody had raked it over or filled in the holes.

She gave Alasdair an apologetic smile and received just a deepening scowl in return. She was in too much of a hurry to worry too much about his feelings, though, she'd just have to make it up to him later with a good bottle of scotch.

She shrugged into the glidewings that he'd had brought for her and leapt up onto the back of the wing, her mechanical legs performing the feat easily without much in the way of effort on her part. She didn't look back at Alasdair as he clambered up behind her, but she just knew that he'd be rolling his eyes at her party trick. Ordinarily she'd climb up the same as everyone else, but every second might count and she was well into her last pre-flight checks when he arrived and strapped her in.

'Thank you, Alasdair. I'll be back soon and, don't worry, I'll land on the airfield.'

Patterson grumbled something under his breath that she didn't quite catch and didn't particularly want to, given the Scotsman's flair for foul-language, then climbed down from the wing. He hurried around the front of the aircraft and she laughed as he shooed away a peacock who'd gotten a little too close, but she didn't wait for him to give her the all-clear and just powered up the spring and cracked the throttle. As soon as the airscrew bit into the air enough to move Kingfisher, she swung her around so that her nose was pointing directly away from the mansion, down the sloping lawn, then pushed the lever through the stops.

Lord Basil Bagshot, Biffy to his wife and closest friends, looked up from his newspaper and the article about the war minister's arrest that had gotten his wife so worked up. Usually the aircraft coming and going from the airfield were too far away to hear beyond a slight buzzing every so often, but for some reason it sounded like there was one right outside and when the windows began to rattle in their frames he rolled his eyes and raised his voice over the noise.

'We have an airfield for a reason, darling!'

With the spring at full emergency unwind and the slight slope in her favour, Kingfisher was accelerating extremely rapidly. However, in her hurry to get to London, Penny had broken a couple of the basic rules every pilot should follow to ensure a safe takeoff. The first, to always takeoff into the wind, wasn't the most important when dealing with an aircraft as powerful as Kingfisher, but the second was one that she was quickly coming to realise she should have paid just a bit more attention to - always always *always* make sure to give yourself enough room.

So, while Kingfisher was fast approaching takeoff speed, she was also fast approaching the trees that separated the gardens from the airfield.

Penelope left it as long as she could, gathering as much speed as possible, then, when she couldn't wait any more, she pulled the stick back into her lap as far as it would go.

Patterson stood at the top of the lawn and watched as the blue aircraft lunged skywards. The undercarriage scraped the tops of the trees, scattering leaves and sending birds fleeing in all directions and he held his breath, expecting the worst. The aircraft didn't get dragged from the sky by the branches, though, and he exhaled in relief, but then her pink nose dropped suddenly and his breath hitched again. He steeled himself, waiting for the sound of the impact and twisting metal, but it never came, instead he caught a brief flash of blue paint before Kingfisher sped into the distance.

'Bloody pilots,' he muttered, shaking his head as he turned to make the long walk back to the airfield.

It was twenty-five miles, as the crow flew, from Bagshot to the centre of London, and, with Penny pushing Kingfisher the whole way, she was over Hyde Airstrip in a matter of minutes. There was barely any air traffic in war time so she flew straight in, taxied right up to the Royal Guard hangar at the south end and left the aircraft in the capable hands of the fitters there.

She had radioed ahead to make sure they knew she was coming and organise transport, but five minutes wasn't enough time for an autocar to be brought from the palace, so she had to make do with the base commander's personal vehicle. It was no great hardship, though, as, like many pilots, the woman enjoyed the sensation of speed on the ground as much as she did in the air and drove a small two-seater autocar that was capable of speeds well in excess of what was legally permitted on the king's highways. It was even painted British racing green, which Penelope heartily approved of.

It took longer to get to the Palace of Westminster than it had done to fly to London, but not by much and, less than twenty minutes after she'd left home, Penelope was striding purposefully through the corridors of power. She breezed past Military Guards, who knew better than to stop her, especially when she had *that* look on her face, and burst into the king's office without knocking.

The king was in one of the two armchairs on either side of a coffee table in the middle of the room and he looked up in surprise.

'George! I'm glad I caught you. A word, please!'

'Penny! What are you doing here? I thought I sent you to Scotland?'

'I'm on leave. The latest squadron has been deployed and I came home while we're waiting for another one to come up. Now, stop changing the subject. Are you going to reinstate the Misfits and, if so, are you going to give me a place?'

'To your first question, I will answer a resounding yes. I am indeed reinstating Misfit Squadron. Have already given the order, in fact. As for the second, I'm afraid you're going to have to ask Abby; it's entirely up to her.'

'Even if Douglas says no?'

'Yes. Even if Sir Douglas Pewtall, the commander of the Royal Aviator Corps, in whom I have absolute trust, says that he doesn't want you to return to the Misfits. Even then. Dame Lennox will have the last say on who she does or does not want in her squadron.'

'Good.' Penny nodded in satisfaction. She waited. Usually, when she burst in, this was when he asked her to sit and take tea. Admittedly, she hadn't burst in on him like this very much in the last year, especially since her accident and, admittedly, she intended to refuse so that she could get back in time to greet her guests, but it was part of their little ritual and rather puzzling that he hadn't done so.

'Well?' The king asked after a moment, looking at her expectantly.

'Well what?'

'Aren't you going to ask her?' He gestured to the armchair in front of him and a head poked around the side.

'Morning, Penny!' Group Captain Dame Abigail Lennox, recently reinstated leader of Misfit Squadron, said with a smile. 'Was there something you wanted?'

Under normal circumstances, Penelope might have been amused, but these weren't normal circumstances and she wasn't in the mood. 'Don't play silly buggers, Abby,' she pointed an accusing finger at the king. 'I get enough of that from him.'

'I resent that!' the king interjected with a grin.

Penelope ignored him and stalked towards Abby. 'Am I in or not?'

'Of course you are, Penny.' Abby said softly, standing up and turning to face her. 'I wouldn't have it any other way. It hasn't been the same without you.'

Abby stepped forward and folded her arms around Penny, who did the same. They held each other, but it wasn't for comfort, it was an acknowledgement of what the moment meant to each of them and what had come before to bring them to this point - the separation, the hardships they'd gone through and, above all, the people they had lost along the way.

When they pulled back, Penny's eyes were burning, but she forced the tears back and kept her emotion out of her voice as much as she could.

'The squadron can have Bagshot Hall again, unless you have other plans.'

Abby smiled. 'That would be wonderful, thank you.'

'How about you come to dinner tonight? You can tell me how you want to go about things.'

'I'd love to.'

'Good.' Penny nodded. 'You can break the news to Biffy, then!' She turned and stalked out, not giving Abby a chance to reply, and closed the door behind herself, muffling the sound of the king's laughter.

Dinners with "the locals", as Lord Bagshot called the gentry who lived in a twenty-mile radius of Bagshot Hall, was a social obligation and therefore necessary, but it was something that he and Penny suffered through, rather than enjoying. More often than not the conversation was inane and of trivial matters and whenever it did turn to current affairs, like the little war that happened to be going on, the participants proved to be so out of touch with reality as to make the Bagshots want to get up and strangle them, or fetch a shotgun.

For Penny, with Abby sitting only a few yards away, that evening wasn't just the usual exercise in combating frustration and biting her tongue, it was torturous. There was so much to discuss and so many plans to make, but not while at the dinner table. It wasn't until eight, when the table was cleared, that the Misfit pilots were able to slip away.

There were many rooms available where they could have sat in comfort, but Abby took them out onto the lawn and away from the house.

They looked up at the stars together for a while, just enjoying the peace and quiet, but they were both so keen to get to work that neither could hold their silence for long.

'Have you spoken to anyone else?' Penny asked.

'I managed to get hold of almost everyone.' Abby replied. 'Everyone that is in the country, at least.'

'So, who do we have?'

'Drake, Tanya and Derek have already said yes. They've enjoyed their time as instructors, but can't wait to get back in the fight. They'll come down from Wales after they've gotten rid of their latest class of recruits. Gwen and Kitty will undoubtedly join us when they get back. Chastity as well, *if* she ever does. Bruce is proving reluctant, though. He likes his new squadron and would quite like to take care of them.'

'That's a shame, but understandable. What about Wendy and Owen?'

'They've said no and I don't blame them. They were never in love with flight like the rest of us, they only went up because it was a way and a means. Now they have their dream assignments there is no need anymore. They have agreed to select and train their replacements, though, and will donate their aircraft to us.'

Penny nodded thoughtfully. 'That's good, if not ideal. That just leaves Scarlet.'

'I couldn't get hold of her to ask her, but I spoke to her commanding officer at the TAS. She's doing some good work and enjoying it a lot, apparently, so she might not want to leave.'

'It wouldn't be the same without her around,' Penny grinned. 'Who would teach us all the colourful local language and find the best places to drink?'

Abby laughed. 'I'm sure we'd manage.'

Penny lowered her gaze from the stars and faced her friend. 'We're going to need replacements, then, but I remember how long it took you to go through all the RAC's personnel files just to find Chastity. I can't imagine how long it would take you to find three or four pilots up to Misfit standards.'

'When the king asked me to form the squadron in 1937,' Abby began, without taking her eyes off the sky, 'many people, particularly politicians, saw it as his folly, a waste of time and money that was better spent on other things. They found out in 1939 how shortsighted that was and how brilliant the king had been. He had created a squadron of aviation enthusiasts - scientists and engineers, clowns and jokers - with brightly-coloured aircraft that they had built themselves, that didn't look particularly threatening and wouldn't give the Prussians an excuse to accelerate their military buildup or derail the efforts of the peace brokers, but that would be in place if war broke out and ready to hold the line while the RAC scrambled to mobilise.'

Abby's eyes were glistening as she continued, emotion cracking her voice. 'Many of those people are gone now and there aren't any enthusiasts left. We've recruited brilliant pilots like Drake, Tanya and Chastity, but no matter how good they are, they're *not* Misfits, not in the way Monty and Mac were. Not in the way Cece was...'

She brought her eyes down and turned to Penny, the tears now streaming down her face. 'The Misfits aren't the Misfits anymore and our aircraft aren't as superior as they once were because Harridans and Spitsteams are getting better with every new variant. Are we even still necessary? Or have we become the waste of time and money that we were accused of being?'

'Of course we're necessary!' Penny insisted fiercely. 'I've seen it. Every new pilot that comes up to Scotland for me to train has a fire in their hearts. They haven't given up hope and they won't, because every single one of them believes that the Misfits will soon rise from the ashes and lead them to victory. We owe it to them and to the country to lead by example and not just fight, but win despite the odds, like we have before, time and time again. And for that we need to be the best - to fly the best aircraft, to have the best pilots. So, shut up, buck up and let's get down to business.'

As if summoned by Penny's words, there was a deep thrum close overhead, the sound of an aircraft's airscrew, and Abby checked her chronograph and smiled.

'You're right, of course, and here comes our first order of business, right on time.'

She wiped her eyes on her sleeve, then took a small flashlight from her pocket and turned it on. She pointed it down at the lawn a few yards in front of her and waved it from side to side, startling a few rabbits from their nocturnal business.

'Are you thinking of recruiting the rabbits?' Penny asked, puzzled at Abby's behaviour.

'Actually, I'm hunting for pixies.'

DROPPING IN

AUGUST 1941

DROPPING IN

'Take a seat, Scarlet.'

'What's this all about, Pip?'

Squadron Leader Philip "Pip" Yaxley was the nominal leader of the Tactical Air Squadron, however, operational command usually fell to Scarlet, who knew the capabilities of the members of the squadron and who would suit which mission best. A summons to Yaxley's office was highly unusual, then and might even be cause for concern. For a moment she thought that her intervention in the Princess of Wales' rescue had come back to bite her; she had technically been absent from her post without permission and had sent another member of her team on a mission without permission or much in the way of notice. Then again... maybe she was being given a medal and a promotion for saving Liz's life. Perhaps she'd even get that sash she had her eye on...

It was none of those things, though, as Yaxley held up what appeared to be a normal mission request slip. 'This just came through. It's all very hush-hush.'

He placed the slip on the table and pushed it across to Scarlet.

The Irishwoman picked it up, expecting the usual fare of information gathering or mild sabotage, but the paper was all but blank - it just set out a takeoff time that night for one of the squadron's Harridan drop aircraft and her name as the assigned operatives.

Scarlet looked a question at Yaxley.

'That's all I can tell you. As I said, it's all very hush-hush.'

Scarlet laughed. 'This isn't just hush-hush, it's mute-mute.'

Yaxley nodded. 'With all the hoohah with the war minister and nobody knowing how far the rot has spread we're going to be changing how we go about our work, cutting down on the number of people who know about the missions and so forth.'

'We've never been exposed before.'

'We don't know that. It might be that the Prussians were told about our work and chose not to act, so that they could continue to receive info and act when it was really important.'

Scarlet tilted her head, conceding the point.

'Anyway,' Yaxley continued. 'Better safe than sorry. Especially with this particular mission.'

'Why, what's so special about it?'

'I can't tell you anything about the specifics, but it's deep cover. For months. You can refuse, of course, but the request has come from the highest levels and for you in particular.'

'The highest levels?'

Yaxley nodded pointedly. 'The highest.'

'Right.' Scarlet said, more to herself than to Yaxley. She stared down at the piece of paper as if it would surrender more details of what she would be getting herself into, but it remained obstinately silent. Mute, even. She chuckled. 'Well, I guess I'd better do it, then.'

Yaxley smiled, rather sadly, Scarlet was quite glad to see. 'Well,' he said, 'you have your equipment ready, I assume?'

'Always.'

'Takeoff is at eight, which gives us plenty of time to see you off.'

The squadron's nature meant that it didn't usually have meals together. They weren't even on the base all at the same time very often. With the army at home there were very little sources of intelligence beyond their operatives and they were kept very busy, either actually on missions, or training for the next one. However, when Scarlet entered the mess that evening, with the exception of a couple of people that were away, everyone was there.

Operatives from the squadron didn't usually get a sendoff before going on missions, but then again none of the missions had ever been of the scope of the one that Scarlet was going on and the squadron, not needing much of an excuse to have a party at the best of times, wasn't going to let the opportunity pass them by.

Scarlet was very well-liked in the squadron. Not only was she always cheerful and joked with all of them, regardless of rank, background, or talent, but almost every single one of them had benefited from her experience in one way or another, resulting in a survival rate far above what had been expected when the squadron had been formed a couple of months ago.

She ate and was as merry as she could be, singing along with all the usual songs and laughing at all the usual stupid jokes, even though she wasn't drinking because of the mission. There was something different about her colleagues that evening, though, a larger than usual light in their eyes and an exuberance above and beyond what there normally was. It wasn't forced, though, as if they were worried for her and putting on a brave face, it was real, as if they were actually happy to see her go. It was strange, but then again the mission was strange, so she thought nothing of it and just concentrated on enjoying herself.

The party was still going when she slipped out, unnoticed, at half past seven and went to her room in the barracks building. She got dressed and picked up her gear and glidewings, then made her way to the squadron's hangar, where she was met by Yaxley, who was standing in front of one of their dark grey Harridans with a small duffel bag at his feet.

'You coming with me, Pip?' Scarlet asked with a grin, jerking her chin at the bag.

Yaxley nudged it with his toe. 'No, this has your orders and a few extra supplies.'

'You're not going to tell me where you're dropping me?'

'I can't. Sorry.'

Scarlet scowled. 'I don't like that.'

'Neither do I, but, if it's any consolation, intelligence puts the closest enemy units at least fifty miles from your drop point.'

Scarlet rolled her eyes. 'Intelligence didn't know there were Prussian agents under their noses in government, how are they going to know where they are on the continent? Frankly, I wouldn't even trust them to tell me there were Prussians in Germany.'

Yaxley laughed. 'They assure me their information is good. You'll be met by some people, apparently, and they'll light your way down.'

'Oh, good. I hope they have the kettle on already, then.' She pick up the bag. 'This is heavy!'

'There are a few things in there to grease palms and sweeten relations. The usual sort of thing.'

'Understood.' Scarlet clipped the bag across her chest, then put on her helmet and goggles.

'Best of British, Scarlet.' Yaxley said, offering her his hand.

'See you soon.' Scarlet said with a grin as she took it. 'Look after my boys and girls.'

'I will.'

Scarlet turned, taking in the dark airfield belonging to the Tactical Air Squadron. She couldn't see the buildings bordering it, but she could hear the raucous party going on in the mess and could picture them easily enough, could picture the people she'd gotten to know over the two short but intense months. She shivered, suddenly strangely sure that she wouldn't ever be back, but quickly pushed the feeling away; doubt would get her killed just as surely as faulty intelligence.

She nodded at Yaxley, then strode past him to the Harridan, where a pilot was already in his seat. She waved at him and got a grin and wave in return, then went to the wing where she was met by four "loaders". She held up her arms as they checked her over, tugging on the various bags clipped to her sneak suit to make sure they were secure and tightening her glidewing straps. When they were satisfied they picked her up, turned her horizontal and carried her under the nearest wing.

In place of guns and cannons, the TAS Harridans were equipped with long thin pods, one under each wing next to the fuselage. She was lifted into one of these and strapped in like plates in the lid of a picnic basket.

'Good luck, ma'am,' their leader said, saluting.

'Thank you.'

She winked at him, then the lid of the pod closed beneath her, plunging her into silence and absolute darkness. There was a small clockwork lamp mounted on the bulkhead above her head, but she didn't turn it on. The TAS operatives called these pods "coffins" with good reason and there were many like Scarlet who preferred to remain in darkness rather than stare at the blank bulkhead a few inches in front of their noses. The claustrophobic conditions were especially hard on those that were nervous about their missions.

After a few seconds there was a sensation of movement as the Harridan started the short taxi onto the airfield, then there were dull thuds and jerks as it began to accelerate over the bumpy grass. The straps holding her in place were ever so slightly elastic, so the ride wasn't as bone shattering as it might have been, but it was still enough to shake her around. Thankfully, it only lasted for a few seconds and then her stomach plunged with the familiar feeling of taking off and the bumping stopped, replaced by gentle swaying as the aircraft was buffeted by air currents.

This part of the flight was where motion sickness claimed the most victims amongst the TAS operatives and they were issued with sick bags because of that. Scarlet never had any problem, though, and just closed her eyes and settled in for the ride, mentally preparing herself to face whatever came, just in case intelligence had gotten things wrong.

'Two minutes to drop.' The pilot's voice sounded in her ear about half an hour later, carried to her by the technically advanced method of a rubber pipe running from the pod to the cockpit.

'Roger! Preparing for drop.'

Scarlet patted herself down, making sure than none of her equipment had come loose with all the shaking on takeoff, then found the release tabs for the straps holding her in the pod.

'Ten seconds to drop. Opening pod.'

'Roger!'

'Good luck, Scarlet.'

'Thanks, Pete.'

The pod swung open beneath her and air rushed in, buffeting her. She searched the darkness for any kind of reference, a light, the moon glistening from a body of water, anything, but it was pitch black, featureless.

This was the bit that frightened Scarlet. Jumping into the unknown. There could be anything below her - the sea, mountains, Prussians, hell, a pit of snakes, for all she knew. She just had to trust that the intelligence people had gotten the landing coordinates right and that the pilot had gotten her to them, because if either party hadn't done their job properly the first she would know about it was when she, quite literally, dropped into it.

It was too late for second thoughts, though, far too late, and when the buzzer went off next to her ear she released the straps with a sharp tug.

The Harridan flew over the channel at top speed, fifteen thousand feet up, so as to be in and out before the Prussians knew it, if they ever knew it. That was far too high for her to float down with the glidewings; it would take an age to get to the ground, so she just let herself fall, watching her chronograph.

After thirty seconds she extended the first two panels of the wings to provide some lift and being to slow her fall. Then, when she felt that her speed had reduced enough, she extended the third panel and in short order the fourth and began to bank around in a circle, searching for a light in the darkness.

She was on her fourth circuit, with the ground getting ever closer, when she finally saw a light being played on the ground a little way off to the side of her. She had plenty of height to spare, but she immediately banked towards it, wanting to get right above it in case it disappeared. It didn't, though, and she settled to the ground right on top of it and folded her wings.

She turned towards the source of the light, but it had gone off and she couldn't see anything beyond a couple of vague shadows.

'Uh, bonswar?'

'Bonsoir.' A female voice called out. 'You are zis fleen? Zee one zey call zee Funny Fairy?'

'It's Pixie,' Scarlet replied, gritting her teeth and walking towards the shadows, 'the Pitiless... oh, never mind. Yes, that's me.'

'Ve 'av been eggspecting you.'

'Good. Now, what's this all about, why am I...' Scarlet frowned as something poked about in the back of her mind and finally found a light switch. 'Hang on.'

A torch appeared in her hand and she swore when she clicked it on to reveal Abby and Penny. Abby grinned and waved, but Penny was doubled over, unable to breathe from trying to hold in her laughter. It finally escaped and she howled, slapping her leg with one hand and clutching at Abby with the other to keep from falling over.

Scarlet put her hands on her hips and glared at them, which only made Penny laugh more.

'Hi, Scarlet!' Abby said cheerfully. 'Glad you could drop in.'

'Abby,' Scarlet nodded, straight-faced. 'I'm not in France, am I?'

'Funnily enough, no.'

'And I'm not going on a mission.'

'No.'

'Can I still kill someone?'

'Not tonight.' Abby eyed Penny, who showed no sign of getting herself back under control. 'Well, not yet anyway.'

'That...' Penny wheezed between sobs, 'was the worst... French ac...French ac... Oh dear... French accent I've ever heard!'

Abby pouted. 'I thought it was rather good actually. I practised it on the flight up. I had Scarlet fooled for a while.'

Penny broke down laughing again.

Scarlet watched her for a while, waiting for her to stop, but when she showed no sign of doing so she looked at Abby. 'Well, I'm fairly sure I can guess why I'm here and where here is, so why don't we get down to it? I'm going to need a drink first, though.'

In response, Abby just clicked her flashlight back on and pointed it at the bag strapped across Scarlet's chest.

Scarlet sighed and ripped open the bag. She wasn't particularly surprised to find that there were no orders and no supplies, instead there was a framed squadron photograph and an extremely good bottle of Irish whiskey cushioned in a silk scarf in County Galway tartan. There was also a note and she opened it and tilted it towards the light.

Scarlet,
We love you dearly and are going to miss you, but you're a Misfit and we don't want you to come back until you've won the war.
Have fun and never stop being you.

The note was signed by every member of the TAS who'd been there that evening and Scarlet laughed; they certainly didn't need her if they'd managed to keep that a secret from her. Especially as she'd been one of the very few people sober.

'Right, then,' she said. 'I'm going to drink a fair amount of this bottle. Once I've done that you can *try* to persuade me to join the Misfits.'

'Haven't you already decided?' Abby asked.

'I had,' Scarlet looked from Abby to the slowly recovering Penelope. 'I'm not so sure I want to now.' She gave Abby an uncharacteristically serious scowl, then stomped past her in the direction of the mansion she now knew was there, leaving her to deal with the lady of the house.

Scarlet found a drawing room that wasn't being used by the dinner guests and took a glass from the side table. She installed herself in an armchair, wrapped her new scarf around her neck and proceeded to empty the bottle of whisky finger by finger.

After half an hour she heard the guests leaving and five minutes later the door opened and Abby and Penelope entered.

Scarlet had arranged the armchairs so that the two of them would be facing her, leaving her in a position of power, but Abby just huffed, poured herself and Penelope drinks from a decanter on the side table and perched on the arm of one of the chairs while Penelope stood beside her.

They had taken the high ground from her, but Scarlet wasn't about to be defeated. She slid down in the chair until she was almost lying down and stared at them insolently as she put her booted feet up on the low table between the armchairs. She held the ridiculous, insolent pose, challenging them, waiting for them to speak.

The two women exchanged a glance, their dismay and doubt plain to see on their faces and Scarlet smirked inwardly at the thought of how much they must have been suffering through the final half an hour of the dinner party. She knew full well how little they both liked formal occasions, especially with the kinds of guests Lord Bagshot would be expected to entertain. The little spanner she had thrown into the works must have made it even worse for them.

'So,' Abby started, 'we would...'

'Of course I'm bloody coming back!' Scarlet cut her off immediately. 'There was never any question!' She jumped up, discarded her glass carelessly on the table and all but leapt onto them. 'Gods! I've missed you!'

She held the hug for what felt like an age, but was still not nearly enough, then pulled back and looked from one of them to the other. 'Now, I assume you've already got back everyone you could, so what are we going to do to make up the numbers?'

'Well,' said Abby, 'Drake says he's got three likely prospects.'

Scarlet's eyebrows rose. 'Three? In one class?'

Abby shrugged. 'You know how that happens sometimes. Anyway, they should be arriving in Scotland for operational training in a couple of days. Why don't we go and have a look at them?'

'Scotland?' Scarlet asked, then sighed and eyed the mostly empty bottle on the table. 'I'd better stock up on decent whiskey then...'

ABOUT THE AUTHOR

Simon Brading's interest in aviation began when he was very young and at thirteen he joined the RAF section of the Combined Cadet Forces of Dulwich College with the aim of becoming a pilot. However, when he was 18, had reached the rank of Flight Sergeant in the CCF and was trying to get into a University Air Squadron, he was told that his eyesight wasn't good enough to be a pilot, so he had to move onto plan B... something else.

He tried his hand at many things before it occurred to him that he might have a few stories to tell. He never lost his interest in flight, though, and hopes to add a PPL to his very basic and probably extremely expired glider license.

www.simonbrading.co.uk

For news of special offers, upcoming releases, exclusive content, competitions and events, please follow me on social media.

Instagram - @sibrading
Facebook - Simon Brading Author
Tiktok - @SimonBradingAuthor

In addition, souvenirs and merchandise, including T-shirts, badges, stickers and more, are available from the Misfit Squadron store on REDBUBBLE at -
https://www.redbubble.com/people/misfitsquadron/shop

ALSO BY SIMON BRADING

The "Displacers" series - a young adult time travel adventure series for all ages.
The Time Traveller's Nephew
The Secret of the Ancients
The Whitechapel Plot
The Price of Greed
The Time for Vengeance

The "Misfit Squadron" Series - a Steampunk series set in an alternate World War 2.
The Battle Over Britain
The Russian Resistance
A Misfit Midwinter
The Lion and the Baron
The Maltese Defence
Tales From the Second Great War
The Siege of Gibraltar
The King's Mission
The Home Front

The Dismal Futures books - stand-alone science fiction tales suitable for adults.
Empath
The Lifeboat at the End of the Universe

The "Twin Ambitions" series - ballet books for children ages 7 and up.
Fight to Dance
Back to Basics

The "Ni Hon - The Two Books" Series - a young adult series set in a dystopian future Japan.
The Black Book

Others
Public Enemy

9 781917 470087